BY JACK GANTOS

Heads or Tails: Stories from the Sixth Grade

Jack's New Power: Stories from a Caribbean Year

Desire Lines

Jack's Black Book

Joey Pigza Swallowed the Key

Jack on the Tracks: Four Seasons of Fifth Grade

Joey Pigza Loses Control

Hole in My Life

What Would Joey Do?

Jack Adrift: Fourth Grade Without a Clue

The Love Curse of the Rumbaughs

I Am Not Joey Pigza

Dead End in Norvelt

From Norvelt to Nowhere

The Key That Swallowed Joey Pigza

The Trouble in Me

THE TROUBLE IN ME

THE TROUBLE IN ME

Farrar Straus Giroux
New York

Farrar Straus Giroux Books for Young Readers
175 Fifth Avenue, New York 10010

Printed in the United States of America
First edition, 2015
10 9 8 7 6 5 4 3 2 1

macteenbooks.com

Library of Congress Cataloging-in-Publication Data

Gantos, Jack.
The trouble in me / Jack Gantos. — First edition.
pages cm
Summary: "Fourteen-year-old Jack falls under the spell of a delinquent Florida neighbor and gets way more trouble than he bargained for"—Provided by publisher.
ISBN 978-0-374-37995-7 (hardback)
ISBN 978-0-374-30345-7 (e-book)
[1. Behavior—Fiction. 2. Juvenile delinquency—Fiction. 3. Friendship—Fiction. 4. Moving, Household—Fiction. 5. Florida—Fiction. 6. Humorous stories.] I. Title.

PZ7.G15334Tr 2015
[Fic]—dc23

2015013115

Farrar Straus Giroux Books for Young Readers may be purchased for business or promotional use. For information on bulk purchases please contact Macmillan Corporate and Premium Sales Department at (800) 221-7945 x5442 or by email at specialmarkets@macmillan.com.

For Anne and Mabel

I must not look on reality as being like myself.

—Paul Éluard

. . . infancy's unconscious spell, boyhood's thoughtless faith, adolescence' doubt (the common doom), then skepticism, then disbelief, then . . .

—Herman Melville, *Moby-Dick*

PREFACE

When I think back on my young-adult years as a drug smuggler, which I wrote about in *Hole in My Life*, I can never say for certain what caused me to abandon my "better self" and impulsively gamble my freedom on a chancy crime that led to my imprisonment. The easy answer is, "I was led astray by the drugs and money." Surely part of that is true. And yet it has to be something deeper than that. Some character flaw that was invisible to me. A small weakness that grew larger as I became a little older.

I was always a liar. But one thing I failed to realize about being a liar is that you know when you are deceiving someone else, but when you deceive yourself you believe you are telling the truth. This is a common deception, and so I grew worse while telling myself I was getting better.

Then two things happened at once, and those two things were like two dry sticks rubbing together to make a flame. I had already gone to five schools in seven grades and had done the best I could at keeping myself on a straight and narrow path. It wasn't easy, but I was toeing the line and I vowed that I would read more books and write more in my journal and this time be ready for eighth grade.

But that summer we suddenly moved again. Maybe this move was just one too many, and at the new house I let myself drift further and further from my books and writing until I gave up on all the smart things I had planned on achieving before school started. Still, I told myself I might get lucky and make a great new friend over the summer—he'd be a popular kid, and he'd help me fit in at my new school. That plan almost worked because for a few summer weeks I did make a great new friend, Gary Pagoda.

Afterward I tried my best to forget him and for a time I had, but then the embers of that summer blazed up inside me. I know I have changed names and other details, but this story is what remains inside of me.

Just by chance Gary was my next-door neighbor and he was everything I had never been. He took me under his wing for only a short time, but he had a powerful effect over me. He showed me how to be his double and learn to love trouble while being cruel and crushing my true self. And that's how I prepared for a different life to begin, by becoming everything I'd never been before.

I told myself that being Gary Pagoda was exactly what I needed. Not fitting in at school was going to be the secret to my success. And that was the truth as I told it to myself, and this is how it played out.

THE TROUBLE IN ME

FIRE

I was still in my white Junior Sea Cadet uniform and was marching stiff-legged like a windup toy across the golden carpet of scorched lawn behind our new rental house. Each splinter of dead grass had once been a soft green blade, but the summer heat had baked them into tanned quills that now crackled like trophy pelts beneath the hard rubber soles of my shoes.

I had one hand holding down my dog-bowl sailor cap, and in the other hand I held a red-and-white tin can of Gulf Lite charcoal lighter fluid. For Dad's birthday party it was my job to fire up the steel grill and I was rushing to get at it.

I would have been sprinting directly toward the grill, but I had outgrown my sailor pants and with each binding stride my thighs rubbed together and made a metallic slicing sound like a butcher sharpening a knife. I had to be careful, because one time I had been running too fast on a bone-dry day and the constant friction generated so much static electricity in my pants that when I accidentally touched my zipper I sent sparks leaping out from my crotch like an electric eel. I shrieked because that really shocked the pus out of me and even splintered a fingernail on one hand. But it was funny, too, because getting zapped between the legs was like some goofy *Popeye* cartoon moment and so I let out a nutty Popeye laugh, "Ah-guh-guh-guh." Dad's nickname for me was Popeye, because that's how I laughed at all his waterlogged navy jokes.

So I was marching out to the grill and hoping not to zap myself below the belt. Another thing about my pants was that they were too short and with each step I could look down and see the tortured leather toecaps of my cadet shoes. My left shoe looked like an aerial-recon photo of Hitler's bunker torn open after the war, and the other looked like a blown-out Tiger tank. "The Commodore"—that's what I called my dad—was always talking about the war and he had told me to put a Popeye spit-shine on my shoes before our morning cadet meeting, but that command went in one ear and out the other and instead I had killed time by drop-kicking chunky fists of white coral across our back canal.

I was trying to punt a hunk through a worn motorcycle tire that loosely swayed from a banyan tree like a black snake masquerading as a knotted noose. Kicking coral was just one of those brainless things I would rather do than do what I was told. A lot of times I found myself doing things where I didn't have to think. I guess it was because thinking always circled me around to dwelling on things that were lousy and painful and generally hateful within myself. For instance, little things—like when my dad said I was lazy or stupid or an idiot or just a knucklehead—got under my skin. I know I shouldn't have been annoyed with him calling me a numb-nut and I should have just shrugged it off, but even though he claimed that calling me names would toughen me up for the "man's world" facing me in the future, his words just eroded the little confidence I had that held the drifty me together.

I don't want you to think I was just being an overly sensitive and spineless kid, so I'll tell you this: one time he called me an ass-wipe and I snapped right back.

"Stop it, for Christ's sake!" I hollered into his face. "You sound like the kids I hate at school."

I don't know why, but my voice always sounded so girly to me when I lost my temper with him. Every time I complained, my voice climbed an octave higher than an Italian soprano's. Of course, that just got him juiced up.

"God, what a *panty* voice you have," he replied derisively, and he laughed in a mocking way at my feeble attempts to sound manly. I hated everything about that word *manly* and what it meant to him. It's like when I played Mitey-Mite football when I was younger and my dad and other dads liked it when we got into fights. They did nothing to stop us. We didn't get hurt because we were wearing so much padding. We'd just bear-hug each other until we twisted over onto the ground and growled into each other's face guard, "I'm going to murder you!"

The dads cheered us on and coached their kid fighters on how to curse other kids with words I won't repeat because most of the filthy ones you know already and don't need to hear them from me.

I didn't play football anymore, but I still had some protective padding left over, only now it defended my heart like a shield. Still, it was impossible to predict when one of Dad's sharp insults would find a chink in my armor. I could be sitting on the edge of my bed with a great book, reading line after line with pleasure, but if even for a second I lifted my eyes from the page and opened my heart to an entrancing passage where I saw myself being heroic, or loved, or brilliant, I was suddenly struck by the escaping memory of one of Dad's lame names for me, like shithead or brain-dead, and my imaginative world wilted away as the printed words bruised and darkened like fruit rotting on a vine.

That's why I was eager to get a blaze going in the grill because somehow, when I stared into the burning flames, it was like having my heart purified of all the ugly words that were lodged within. It was a relief to unlock the full chambers of my heart and feel that no cruel words in the world could harm me. I think some of you know what I mean by that—maybe all of you know what I mean.

But some good-boy part of me must have wished I did polish my shoes as Dad had ordered because I suddenly fixed my eyes so intently on the chalky, gouged-up leather that I had time to imagine my dad yanking one shoe off my foot and with a screw gun mounting it upright atop one of those cheap brassy-assed trophy columns you find lined up in high school corridors, only my trophy would be on display beneath a vitrine in our living room where a crisp white note card pinned to the wall would read JACK'S CRAPPY MILITARY DRESS SHOE, 1964. This trophy would mark just one more of the accomplishments lining the hallways of my imaginary Museum of Mockery and would remind me each day that I hadn't yet achieved anything my father thought was *really* "trophy-worthy." He loved that two-word phrase, and when it came out of his mouth it could be a buttery pat-on-the-back compliment for getting an A on an American history test, or it could be so sarcastic and belittling that I'd slink back to my room and curl up on the bed like a fishhook and cry until I was rusty.

He could be rough with his words, but he wasn't a hitting dad. Hitting dads are a menace, and that old black rubber noose hanging across the water was a reminder that some guys grow up to be meaner than their dads. A friend I didn't see anymore from my old South Miami neighborhood told me his dad was a *hitter.*

"It's not like I do anything too wrong," my friend had said with a shrug one day as we played catch with his dad's signed Mickey Mantle baseball. "He just gets pissed off at stupid little shit. I know when he's going to go mental because his lips turn purple and get as puckery as a dog's butt-hole, and then he whips around and hits me."

The kid and I got some small green scuff marks on the Mantle ball from where it hit the grass a few times. In his garage I watched as he nervously tried to fade them away with a Q-tip dipped in bleach, but his hand slipped and he blurred part of Mantle's autograph.

"Anyway, the signature is a fake," the kid revealed. "My dad bought it at a flea market and he shows it off like it's real. But I bet he kicks my ass anyway."

He reared back and fired the ball down the concrete driveway to the rough asphalt road.

"What the heck," he said as we watched the ball hit hard, then bounce a few times until it ticked off the raised lip of a sewer cover and veered into someone's front yard. He left it there.

A few days later his dad did kick his ass. I heard through his older brother that it was a nasty belt-buckle beating. I meant to go over and say something sympathetic to him because I was the one dropping the ball in the grass, but I never did and soon my dad's roof-whitening business fell apart as my mom predicted it would and we suddenly moved away and I never saw the kid again. I wasn't really worried about him, though. He was one of those guys who might pack a bag one day and walk out of his house and down to the train station and hop a freight and never be seen again. He was a pretty good kid, and real smart, and I think he knew he had to leave home if he wanted to stay that way. He read a lot and knew a lot of cool stuff, and I used to dream that maybe he could have lived with us—not as a brother but just as a good friend. We could have made each other better and avoided the dumb stuff by doing the right stuff.

But I never bothered asking my parents. They wouldn't ever have gone for something like that—especially now that we had the baby coming so no extra expenses were allowed, and kids were an expense. Even the dog I was promised was now crossed off the list as an extra expense.

Aside from being a "mouth bully" my dad was okay. He could control his hands if he got overheated. Besides, now that I imagined the nutty mocking shoe trophy, it put me in a silly mood, and in a goofy way I kind of liked the trophy idea and I decided I should make one for my room. I could use a golf shoe and make a crazy back-scratcher trophy, only in my case I'd use it to kick myself in the ass when I needed to get a move on—like right now—because I really had to get the charcoal grill started.

"Jesus, Jack, you are so frigging slow!" I muttered.

Sometimes I talked to myself in the same salty way my dad talked to me, and it did me some good because he was just trying to keep me on the straight and narrow. I figured people had to be tough on me because when they were too nice I didn't listen to them. I was an okay kid, but I cut corners on just about everything. You'll see.

Anyway, it was hard for me to respect people who thought I was a great kid just because I wore a sailor outfit. They were really missing the boat if they didn't see I was as two-faced as fire. With the flip of a coin I could cause pleasure or pain. If they knew what kind of mindless junk I was really thinking about all day long they'd change their opinions about me—especially if they knew what a snake I was with pretending I was someone I was not. I was really sort of a drifty kid who was lost at sea, you might say. "Easily led off course," was how my sister nicely put it. If I had to write an essay on the subject I'd put it this way: I was really good at faking I was cruel when it suited me to feel cold and unkind inside. I say *faking* because later on I felt incredibly sick and guilty about doing some of the awful things I'll tell you about, where a *truly* cruel person wouldn't give a shit about a sentiment as pussy as guilt.

Of course, I also had days when it suited me to be overly kind to some person in order to sway them into liking me. At those times I was pretty genuine about my friendship. I guess you could boil it down to saying I was just a kid who was nice around nice kids and cruel around cruel kids. My mom always advised me that it was better to always "be yourself," but if you didn't like yourself then, believe me, it was better to be someone else you could tolerate. No matter who I thought I was, good or bad, I aimed to please. Like I said, you'll see.

Anyway, despite my tight pants I figured out how to prance sideways across the crunchy grass like I was a pair of sewing scissors doing some kind of yodeling Alpine folk dance. Since it was Dad's birthday I was determined to help pull off something spectacular for him and give him a "trophy moment," as he called the few really perfect things that our family managed to put together for him.

Dad was working a new job selling concrete products. He had been in the navy during the war and was now the commander of our Sea Cadet chapter and had high standards of perfection on land and sea. If Noah had finally washed up on Fort Lauderdale Beach in his rudderless ark after a couple thousand years of bobbing around like a cork, Dad would have had him court-martialed and keel-hauled for his crummy seamanship. But that's how Dad was—his spit-shined years in the navy trained him to find the flaws in life. To be fair, he found the whole world flawed, but as they say, the greatest flaws are in your own backyard, and that is where I could be found cutting a dandy path across the dead splinters of grass as I snipped this way and that toward an unknown disaster.

Today I was determined to help give him the flawless gold standard of trophy moments so that he could brag about it to all his naval officer buddies.

At our morning cadet meeting I had taught new recruits how to read naval alphabet flags and spell out distress messages like CAPTAIN AHAB GONE MAD and BLACK PLAGUE ON BOARD and MUTINY ON THE MIDSHIP. Dad had taught me all the flags on signalman flash cards when I was younger and it had inspired me to make something very ego-polishing for him that I was sure he'd admire.

The moment we returned home from our meeting Mom was ready for him. Before Dad could shift our

Rambler Classic into park she shuffled out of the house in her pink lounge shoes and sent him in reverse on some cooked-up pharmacy chore to buy us time to organize the final details of his surprise party. She was pregnant and showing pretty big now, but he was the one more puffed up with pride. Still, he was taking instructions from her on the double.

I quickly hopped out of the Rambler before I got trapped in it. As he zoomed off he tilted his head out the window and hollered back to her, "Your wish is my command!"

The Rambler's water-pump bearing was squealing at such a high pitch it was hard to hear his theatrical exit.

But she had heard it and she stood quietly with the fingers of her hand spread open like a starfish across her stomach and a bit-lip look on her face like when she was stumped on a crossword puzzle question. She was going to have to quit her job at the bank and she was probably trying to think up the word for the crossword clue that asked, "Who pays the bills?"

Maybe she was reviewing her secret wishful-thinking museum full of "things could be better" trophies. People always said she and I were alike. We didn't look alike, but somehow people saw in us the similarities we couldn't seem to share between ourselves. Scratch that last thought. She probably saw the similarities all too well and was appalled by them. I was the one who was blinded to them, seeing as I'm always so self-involved, as everyone is still quick to point out.

At that moment, while she stood there sorting out the crossword puzzle that was our family, I didn't have time to wonder what her wishes might be. I had work to do and that's when I had retrieved the charcoal lighter fluid from the garage shelf and stiffly marched toward the back of the house.

Mom had put me in charge of setting up the grill for the cookout because I was a pro at it, and as I now frolicked this way and that across our wide backyard in my crotch-shocking too-tight pants I put my whole body in motion. I felt good. Fire was in my future. I picked up speed, then more speed until I was skipping like a flat stone across the slick surface of the polished grass while my thoughts trailed behind me like a string of alphabet flags whipping sharply in the wind. Maybe those flags spelled out STORM WARNING and signaled me to slow down and consider the danger ahead, but I was in no mood to think about the perilous course I was setting.

In fact, thinking ahead never helped me much. Thinking on my feet worked best. Things happened and I reacted. That perfectly describes my version of thinking, which was not thinking insomuch as it was just stimulus-response instincts. I should have a knee-jerk trophy for that. It would look like a tiny squirrel brain mounted on the tip of a vibrating stick.

I was going full speed ahead across the yard and directly in my path was a hip-high concrete planter of stoic-faced Chief Osceola. I could have altered my course and navigated around the great-leader-turned-planter, but instead I leaped over him like a light-hearted singing sailor. The chief was holding a pot of wilted hibiscus and when the slick rubber sole of my back shoe slipped on the dry grass, my front shoe came down short and I cracked my ankle against Osceola's rock-hard shoulder.

I tumbled over just once, then sprang neatly back up onto my feet as if my fall were a stunt I was practicing for the coming Olympics. I was fine. As I adjusted the dog bowl on my head I looked toward our back porch to see if my mother or sister might have caught that act. No one had. Perfection always struck me when no one was paying attention.

Still, my mom would figure out that something had happened because now I was covered with brittle needles of dried-up grass that had pierced my swabbie outfit, and as I plucked out each sharp blade a thin red dot of blood pooled up on the white cotton uniform. I sort of looked like a game bird that had been winged here and there with a load of miniature birdshot. But I was alive.

My ankle throbbed and I lifted my foot and rubbed the sore spot while I stood on my other foot like a dizzy flamingo. I was twitching about and hopping side to side from shifting my weight around to maintain my balance. Sweat pooled between my shoulders and a salty stream slipped like a zipper down my back. At that moment I seemed to step out of my own skin as if stepping out of a costume.

Overhead the glowing face of the Florida sun hovered like a stopped clock. I squinted upward and as I did so the thick, honeyed rays of light began to drape down around me like a slowly descending bell jar until I felt like a captive specimen under that airless amber glass. I looked down at my shadow as if I were my own sundial. I guessed it was sometime after two o'clock but not quite three—the hottest time of the day. The "blast-furnace" time of the day, the weatherman called it, because the scorching heat thinned the rising air. Old people stayed indoors breathing in and out of their oxygen tubes and then switching off to drink cold Key lime daiquiris through plastic straws. On especially hot days jets were grounded at Fort Lauderdale Airport because the air wasn't dense enough for liftoff. After blast-furnace days like this there were always extra columns of obituaries listed in the newspaper of the old folks who didn't survive the asphyxiating atmosphere.

Sometimes my mother and I read the obits out loud to each other. So many of the old people had been born in Europe.

One day, in the middle of reading about a woman from Warsaw, she closed her eyes and lowered the paper. "It's just awful," she said grimly. "This state is a graveyard for concentration camp survivors. God knows, after what they've been through they deserve better than this . . . this . . ."

She pawed her hand over the tabletop as if paging through a dictionary for the right word. "This . . . crematorium," she said, settling regretfully on the word she both wanted and didn't want.

I didn't know what to say. The cruelty was unbearable to imagine. How fair was a life where you escaped Hitler's fires but died of heatstroke?

My mother looked directly into my eyes. Her sadness entered me in a glance and pinned me down.

My eyes watered over and I lowered my chin and silently cried. I was no match for the depth of her grief and crumbled beneath it.

But now I had to get a move on. I needed that grill fire to heal me within. My heart was aching for it. I put one hand on Chief Osceola to steady myself as I lowered my sore foot onto the grass. I bent over at the waist with my hands on my wobbly knees. I could breathe easier that way. Maybe I had hurt myself more than I realized. Maybe I had hit my head when I took a tumble, or maybe the heat was getting to me.

I could probably use a glass of water. The ocean breeze had brought the humidity that was so thick the flies slowly circled around my face like winded swimmers. I reached up and plucked them out of the air as if they were blackberries on a bush. I slowly closed my hands. I didn't crush them. They buzzed until they didn't. I lumbered down to the brackish edge of the canal we lived on. The water was so sluggish and thick with some invasive African algae it smelled like steaming muck. Or maybe the canal had died long ago and the foul, gelatinous muck was the stranded carcass of the living water that had once thrived there.

Now only the most toxic fish survived in it. Actually, they didn't swim as much as they tunneled their way forward like spoons in chocolate pudding.

I flicked the flies onto the surface. Instantly the red mouth of a black snakehead took them under. Snakeheads were evil fish from Korea that seemingly had chewed their way through the center of the earth and had taken over the Florida canals. Swarms of them would attack and eat small alligators. They could even live on land. At night they slithered out of the muddy sludge and flopped around like spastic zombie fish searching the neighborhood for prey. In the morning you had to be careful when walking by the damp shrubs because they hid under the low hibiscus leaves and could spring forward and attack your feet or the mushroom-soft nose of a sniffing dog. I asked Dad for a speargun so I could shoot them, but he said I'd just hurt myself. Maybe.

I stood by the canal and wiped the fly bits from my hands onto my pants. I was a believer that every living thing was an important link in the chain of life, but I hated those snakeheads. Humans were supposed to be on a higher rung than others, but at the moment I didn't feel like a shining example of a half-boy, half-man. I was fourteen but closer to being thirteen than fifteen. Or that's how my mother put it. She gave me the late-bloomer trophy, which in her mind probably looked like a big peanut that would never be mature enough to outgrow its own shell.

Whatever. I really had to get a move on. My father wouldn't be gone that long. The new pharmacy was in a strip mall about a half mile away next to the army-navy surplus store I liked to visit. So many kids had stolen stuff from the store that if you weren't with a parent you had to get permission from the reluctant owner before you could come in and shop. He'd pat you down with his hard hands on the way out. Who could blame him? The kids in this sketchy neighborhood were known as thieves.

Anyway, I'd go there to shop for rare stuff like bravery-under-fire medals that I hadn't earned. But mostly I liked to slowly patrol the aisles and smell all the useless stuff like rubberized gas masks, moth-eaten flight jackets, and boxes of broken chocolate bars covered in powdery white sugar bloom. All the military hardware had been lightly sprayed with machine oil to keep it from rotting. When I breathed through my mouth I could faintly taste the merchandise-flavored oil on the shelf in front of me. The distinctive flavor gave each object a realistic purpose and I could easily pretend I was in the war.

One time when shopping in the enemy-army surplus section, I had closed my eyes and when I breathed deeply I inhaled the horsey odor of Wehrmacht leather and imagined that was my final smell while kneeling before the polished boots of a German officer. He aimed a Luger at my head. He clicked off the safety and pulled the trigger. I tried to make myself pass out in the store from the imaginary pain. Instead, I lost my balance and tilted face-first into the metal edge of a display shelf. I cut a notch out of my forehead that produced a trickle of blood. It was like the bullet had bounced off my thick skull.

I loved playing in that warehouse museum of war supplies, and was just thinking about it when a squealing car turned onto my street. I thought it was my dad, but it wasn't. Broken water pumps were common in Ramblers.

My banged-up ankle felt a little better. I limped over to the grill and dragged it, and a bag of charcoal, from our side of the galvanized chain-link fence that separated us from the Pagoda family next door.

I set everything along the narrow streak of shade between two coconut palms. I filled the metal bowl of the grill until I had a rough pyramid of briquettes. Then I went back to the planter and picked up the can of lighter fluid. It had slipped out of my grip when I fell because the palms of my hands were sweating. I picked it up again. It slipped out a second time. So I used two hands this time. That's called thinking.

I doubled back to the grill and squirted the entire can of lighter fluid onto the coals. That can had annoyed me, and with my two hands I squeezed out every wheezing last drop until I had flattened the sides together as if I had crushed its flimsy neck. The coals were so saturated with lighter fluid they began to look like huge, winking black jewels dripping with oily rainbows along their waxy edges. I wondered if they might spontaneously combust because of the heat. That was sort of a brain-dead question, but stepping out from the shadow of that dumb question was the untested notion that if I did something theatrical I might just jolt myself from the stupor of my lousy mood and get back into the birthday-party spirit.

So I took the theatrical test I had in mind. I leaned back from the grill, and with one hand tossed the empty can end over end into the canal. With my other hand I tugged a pack of wooden matches from the back pocket of my uniform. In one motion I struck a match and flicked it lazily toward the grill. The match arced through the air like a tiny toy torch thrown by a tiny toy soldier at a tiny toy castle, and then before it reached the grill it vaporized as the *whoosh* of an Old Testament fireball hit me full on.

THE FOLLOWER

I had to have yelled out an unmanly scream as I quickly covered my face and dropped down to one knee. The red blossom of heat puckered the skin along my forearm, and as the flame sucked back into itself I lowered my arm to look at the damage. In an instant a colony of small milky blisters appeared from my wrist to my elbow. I smelled burning hair and fuel as if I were a soldier trapped in a shell-punctured tank.

My heart pounded. *Wow*, I thought, *that perked me up!*

I was grinning and laughing hysterically with my crazy Popeye "guh-guh" laugh, which I hadn't felt inside me for a good, long while. The last two months I had fallen into a gloomy rut. But that was suddenly over. I was laughing again. I danced around and thrust out my legs, jabbing them left and right as if I had just karate-kicked open the golden door to eternal happiness. I was snorting out my nose.

"Oh my God!" I shouted up into the sky. "I *love* fire!"

I slapped at myself. Smoke drifted off my clothing and hair and I felt alive. Nothing, it seemed to me, had ever wanted me more than those flames whose healing hot hands seized me by the shoulders and ordered me to "Wake up!" and I wanted nothing more than to be fully awake, and unexpectedly it occurred to me that I had never closed my eyes and slowly kissed a girl on the lips.

Why did I think that?

If inhaling a storm cloud of flame was what a kiss would feel like, then I was ready to try finding a girl to kiss, but girls always looked at me and turned away as if I were the immature boyfriend they had outgrown and discarded. The closest I got to feeling their hands on me was when they held a pencil and scratched my name off a list of possibilities.

So I turned to where I was always wanted and stared wide-eyed into the unwavering column of beautiful dancing flames that thrust upward from the grill as if a rocket had crashed in front of me like a dart into the dirt and the engine was still roaring full blast. The thrusting flames stood out like bloodred bayonets of molten steel. The power of those flames was purifying. Staring into them set the canyons of my mind on fire and charred the weedy debris of dead thoughts. Flames were a natural language more powerful than the chaos of wind or water. Flames wanted to renew a world that had become tiresome and I wanted my tiresome world to be renewed. Even the wounded chambers of my heart, cleansed of all my father's awful insults, relaxed into a much-needed sleep. At that moment my dreams felt stronger than my weaknesses.

After a minute those glowing pickets of flame began to lower, and above them I could see a devil's ruddy, heat-wavering face and it was leaning forward and staring directly into mine. He had red-hot hair that glistened with oily sweat. It was cut short except in the front where it curled onto his forehead like a burnished copper wave breaking down over his eyes and nose and mouth. As the flames further declined I saw his red neck and shirtless chest and his open black leather motorcycle jacket with glinting silver snaps and diagonal zippers all as liquid bright as mercury, and below the dangling leather belt buckle was the elastic waistband of a pair of boys' undershorts with SEARS stretched across the top, and below the undershorts were two skinny red-haired rooster legs with just one white pointy leather shoe cocked over the top edge of a short garden pitchfork.

He pushed his hair back to where I could see his face and he was having a good laugh at my expense. He wasn't tall but he was muscular enough, and when he lifted and stabbed the pitchfork into the earth he grunted and then levered up a damp clod of sandy clay, swiveled around, and tossed it aimlessly over his shoulder. The chunk of dirt did a cannonball right into their swimming pool. He didn't care to notice. He kept staring at me as if I were his trophy and he was digging a tunnel to hell and at any moment he was going to take me with him.

Then, as the flames crouched down onto the coals like little dancing ghosts, his face remained and I realized he was a real person and not some overheated hallucination. It had to be Gary Pagoda, the mysterious next-door neighbor my mother had warned me about. She had seen him escorted to his front door by a man in a blue suit. They had driven up in a patrol car with a door logo that read BROWARD COUNTY JUVENILE PROBATION.

I hadn't met Gary yet, but the other day when I was mixing a batch of homemade navy napalm by slowly stirring gasoline into a jar of Vaseline I had heard what I figured was his mother's husky voice holler out the window, "Gary, you get back here and finish filling out these forms!"

I remembered the moment clearly because it happened just as I was sucking the napalm up into a turkey baster and squirting a thick stream into the conical opening of a crusty termitary tower.

"If you don't straighten up," she continued, "and take your paperwork to your juvie group session, your probation officer is gonna jerk your butt back in jail!"

Gary was standing on his front lawn and his eyes were fixed on a white Ford pickup that had pulled a crisp U-turn in front of his house. A blond girl was driving. She waved to him and smiled. No girl had ever smiled at *me* with such sunny and almighty intentions. It left an impression on me.

"Did you hear me!" his mother continued as I lit the termite cone on fire.

Of course he heard his mother. We all had. But Gary's black leather profile was like an eclipse that slowly changed day into night as he passed between his house and the clean white truck. He never answered his mother and without hesitation he raised his middle finger straight up and corked it tight into the eye of the sun. He stood there grinning in triumph and then he lowered his arm until the shadow of that finger stretched across the lawn like the needle of a compass and pointed directly into the cab of the truck. At that moment the girl kicked open the passenger door and reached out with both of her slender tan arms toward his glowing face. *That* was a golden-armed trophy moment for him.

But not for me. Or for the termites who died for no other reason than I liked to hear their chitinous exoskeletons go *pop!*

Now I continued to stand in front of my blistering grill as Gary stopped shoveling and pointed a finger at me and laughed his ass off. I could smell something burning. In a panic I looked down at my uniform and whirled around and wildly slapped at myself while fearing I was on fire. I turned back toward him.

"What?" I hollered with the palms of my hands spread open in alarm. "What?"

He just kept pointing.

"Just tell me!" I called out with more desperation. "What?"

He raised his finger and pointed above my head.

"Oh, crap!" I shouted as I snapped my head up and saw what I knew I would. Before Dad and I left the house that morning I had arranged for my older sister to tie a banner I had made of fancy gold-edged naval alphabet flags copied from the nineteenth-century USS *Pennsylvania* that spelled out HAPPY BIRTHDAY COMMODORE between the palm trees. Now the banner was furiously on fire from the oil paint I had used on the flags and it was nosing downward on one end like the flaming *Hindenburg*.

"Noooo!" I cried out, painfully realizing that my trophy moment was going up in smoke on its way down to the ground, and there was no chance I was going to re-create it and impress my father, who puffed out his chest when we all saluted him and addressed him as "Commodore." The ladder was still against a tree trunk, and quick as a monkey I scrambled up the rungs and reached out and yanked down the laundry rope of burning flags. I jumped from the ladder and hit the ground and did a somersault and yelped again because of the dang sharp grass needles, but I didn't have time to cry about it because I had to fold up the smoldering banner of painted cardboard before one little spark set the whole dry grass yard into a blazing inferno. So I moved quick as a cat and with my stinging hands rolled the banner up into a large wad of cardboard and rope and in one swift moment picked it up and ran toward the canal, where I threw it overhead as far as possible. It didn't go far. The smoldering ball slowly fluttered down into a loose heap of fallen puppetry on the starter fluid can. There must have been enough fluid left to leak out and form an oily slick on the muck, and the next thing I knew a circle of flames flared up around the can and the banner. I stood there wondering what I might do next to put out the fire and get rid of the evidence.

I wished we had a garden hose and the next thing I knew Gary was at the edge of the canal, just on his side of the fence. I looked over at him and thought that this was a bad time to start a conversation and introduce myself. Not only was my uniform scorched and bloody and my arms singed and blistered, but there he stood with his undershorts pulled down, and he was leisurely taking a leak into the water.

"Do you have a hose?" I blurted out in a half-mad way while thinking I should just return to the grill. I didn't belong there while he was doing what he did.

He shrugged and pointed to the burning banner with his chin. "It's out of my range," he replied. "Besides, I really like fire. Like, *really*." His red eyebrows peaked upward like fox ears eavesdropping on prey. "I wouldn't put it out," he said, "not even if I was hung like a horse."

That was the kind of seaman's talk my dad's navy friends used at their officers' club and hearing it so casually from Gary was unexpected and I snorted through my nose.

I was naturally shy and I avoided his eyes and coughed and looked down at his skinny chicken legs covered with wiry red hairs above his pointy white shoes. I didn't yet know the shoes were fake alligator or that they were called X-15s after the hypersonic jet. I didn't know his motorcycle jacket was a real Harley-Davidson jacket. In fact I didn't know anything about cool shoes or jackets or motorcycles or tow trucks or fireworks or cigarettes or girlfriends who drive trucks or whiskey or gangs or stealing cars or secret clubhouses or love or prison or soul music or real cruelty or anything like that. But in an instant everything I did know seemed childish and I was suddenly in a rush to catch up to everything he knew and felt.

He was what I wasn't, but in an instant I intended to become what he was. All that longing to be like him set something inside of me on fire and I had a feeling that there was no putting me out.

He peed for so long I got nervous and kept glancing toward the screen door in back of my house. If my mother came out from the kitchen with some party food and saw him with his shorts down she would say something. She wouldn't be nasty, but she would have no hesitation in calmly pointing out that he was outside, half naked, and peeing in public, which was unsanitary, especially when people were cooking and eating only a few feet away on the other side of a wire fence that germs could easily pass through. She had a thing about migrating germs. She still feared the invisible spread of polio.

But he finished first, took a deep breath, shook himself off, and pulled up his undershorts just before Mom opened the back door.

"Jackie!" she called out, sniffing left and right as she scanned the yard. "Do you smell something burning?"

I turned to Gary. "Don't tell my mother anything," I said in a half whisper. "She won't understand."

"*Understanding* is what you want from your girlfriend," he sagely replied, and for emphasis he slowly zipped and unzipped the tracks of silver teeth on his leather jacket. "*Control*," he said with contempt, "is what your parents want from you. Tattoo that on your sailor beanie and sign it *Gary Pagoda*."

I wouldn't do that. Not exactly. But much later I would write down in a notebook what he said, and then I followed his words with my own words, which were as permanent as a tattoo. I wrote, "This is the day I realized that the unknown self deep within me is the self to pursue, and that the known self is the superficial self I have to burn all the way down to the ground without ever looking back."

"Jackie!" Mom called again.

"*Jackie*," he quickly mimicked, then added in a mincing voice, "Isn't *Jackie* a girl's name?"

I suddenly hated that junior version of my name. I turned from him and looked toward her.

"Is the grill ready?" she called out.

"Is the *girll* ready?" he mimicked just loud enough for me to hear.

I nodded. "Yep," I called back to Mom.

"Then don't just stand there," she said impatiently. "Come get the hamburgers! He'll be home at any moment."

I lurched toward her, but instead of landing with my shoe on the dry grass I seemed to step onto that narrow platform of white space that both separates and connects the train of printed words. Instantly I sensed that I was no longer myself. Something had changed when I met Gary and I no longer felt trapped by a past that judged me. I was escaping my old self, and now I was riding a fresh train of words that would transport me toward that unknown secret new self.

Those words I was riding were as solid to me as if I had been racing a train full speed along the railroad tracks. As it rumbled past me I reached up with one hand, gripped a metal handle on the corner of a car, swung my feet upward, and in a perfect arc hopped right onto the clanging iron coupling between the freight cars that were hauling boxes of words that would spell the story of my new life. That train sped me away so swiftly I didn't have time to look over my shoulder and miss myself. I think that's the moment I gave myself away. As my mother later said, after I was escorted home from custody and we hastily moved to a better neighborhood, "You gave yourself away for cheap. For *nothing*."

But she was wrong. It was the moment I got carried away and in an instant became everything I had ever wanted from myself—and a lot more than I guessed I had in me. And who knows, maybe I wanted the trouble, too. I didn't see it coming, but the moment it showed up and said "Follow me" that is just what I did. It's the moment when I became "the follower." I was Gary's follower. He was Peter Pan and I was his shadow, and his words replaced my words and his emotions were now my emotions. His choices were now my choices. His way of doing things was now my way.

They say you can never escape your past because it is always hiding like a conscience within your present, but in my case the present had no past. I had hopped onto Gary's train and now I was living every second in *his* present and my future was going to have to think on his two feet.

TROPHY MOMENT

Dad was turning thirty-eight. Last year, while framing a house, he had cut off half his left-hand index finger with a circular Skilsaw. Around that time Jack Ruby had shot and killed Lee Harvey Oswald with a snub-nosed .38 and Dad had nicknamed himself "Jack Ruby."

At breakfast on his birthday morning he had aimed his stubby trigger finger at us and said, "*Blam, blam.* You'll be gunned down on live TV like that assassin Oswald if I don't get my big you-know-what party tonight."

He laughed and I laughed, too, just to go along with him, but not for long. Mom stiffened and declared that he should never refer to "that horrid Ruby man again" or decent people would find Dad "just as *contemptible.*" Every time Mom used a four-syllable word she said it as if it were always *italicized.*

She had admired President Kennedy, who, like me and Dad, was named John but called Jack. She especially loved Jackie Kennedy because she, too, was a mother with young children and my mom wiped tears from her eyes whenever the brave Kennedy children, Caroline and John-John, were shown on TV.

Mom had a tender inner life, which I feared because instinctively I knew her kind heart had given birth to my own heart and I had her same softness within me, but I was a boy and not a mom and it seemed impossible, even wrong, that we could share the same emotional life. Still, we did, though tenderheartedness expressed itself differently through us.

For her, sadness was a mood that connected her to an embracing world of others who were equally sad and equally resolute.

For me, sadness was a repulsive flaw I hid darkly within myself so I couldn't find it. I was ashamed of my sadness and knew it was a sign that I was not brave; instead I was a coward, and being a coward was the source of the whole world's scorn.

How could sadness give her great strength when it only left me feeling weak and small? I loved my mother and it confused me to think that this difference in our twin hearts might tear us apart.

When I left Gary standing at the canal and ran up to thc back porch to get the tray of hamburgers and buns from my mother, she firmly looked me in the eye and said to me, “Let’s make sure this is a special moment for your father. He works very hard, and I want this party to make him proud of his family.”

“I hear you loud and clear,” I replied, and gave her a snap salute, then quickly took the tray and turned away from her before she noticed my bloody shirt and blisters. The tray was heavy in my hands, but even a cloud would have been heavy in my hands at that instant because I was feeling gutless and weak for not telling her I had already ruined the trophy moment by setting the special banner of honorific flags on fire.

“No monkey business,” she warned as I marched away.

“Okay,” I called back earnestly. “I promise I’ll do a good job on the grill.” I truly was sorry about the burned flags and wanted to make up for the stupid blunder.

But when I returned to the grill and stared down into the eyes of the glowing coals, they leaped up like red bolts of lightning and seared that dutiful promise right out of my mind. I removed the hamburgers and buns from the tray and hastily tossed them any which way onto the scorching grate. Almost instantly the meat drippings and snotty gobs of fat sizzled and crisped like someone burning at the stake, but I wasn't paying them any attention.

I just stood there in a glazed trance while watching Gary dig the hole in his backyard. I was traveling on his train now and I knew it. Where he went and what he did mattered most. My time was now. My mother and father were losing their influence over me. When I looked at them I could see that their own teenage dreams had expired. Maybe they had had bigger plans that melted away with their wasted days and nights. And once they had us kids, their chances for greatness became as extinct as dinosaurs and now they just wanted to survive. Their past was not a story I wanted to live. This day was my turn at greatness. I was the young one now, and Gary was my leader. I was following him out of the dull trap of my life. Soon, I knew, I would catch up and be equal to him. Then I would be him. Then maybe I would surpass him. And he would want to be like me. He would envy me because I would be the stronger leader and he would be the follower.

That was what I was thinking as my eyes were glued on Gary and my neglected party food burned into furiously charred fists on the grill.

He kept digging and every now and again his mother pulled a window curtain to one side. She coughed and exhaled empty clouds of gray cigarette smoke that were abruptly filled with tarred words. “Is the hole finished yet?” she hollered in her raspy voice.

Gary shrugged. “No,” he said patiently. “Give me a minute.”

In less than a minute she hollered out, “Are you digging to the center of God’s unholy earth?”

“I would,” he replied sarcastically, “if I could be sure I’d find your big ol’ fat hunk of bacon down there.”

“Then what’s taking so long?” she called back, clearly annoyed.

“For God’s sake, Mom,” he replied in frustration, and jammed the garden fork into the ground. “You’re puttin’ me in a bad mood and you know how I can get when I’m in a *mood*.”

“You’re always in a *mood*,” she whined, imitating him.

“It’s a greyhound we are burying,” he said. “It’s the size of a four-legged third grader.”

“Maybe we could use the *grave* your probation officer said you already dug for yourself,” she suggested in a clever voice meant to needle him. “He said it’s dug pretty darn deep after all your sass and law-breaking stunts.”

"I figure we'll save that grave for the future," he replied slickly, "so when I'm dead you can roll me into it and kick the dirt over my smiling face with your slippers."

"Don't you dare turn your moody smart-ass mouth onto me," she threatened. "Or I'll call your officer in a jiffy and give him an earful—don't think I don't know that you sneak out at night for God-knows-what trouble."

"A little fresh air is good for my health," he replied. "And fresh air would be good for yours, too."

"And being fresh with me is bad for your health," she said. "Now, dig!"

Their conversation carried back and forth like they were an old married couple gnawing on words that could never nourish love. I only found out later that she lived entirely in the house. Gary said she was a freakishly big woman who never went outside and when she walked the halls the whole house rocked back and forth like it was a boat tied to a dock.

I wasn't sure why she never went outside—vanity or insanity, I figured. But with the Pagoda family there was no reason why they did anything and yet they were always doing something. The five of them just did what they wanted. They were all loudly critical of each other. Our houses were so close I could hear most everything, but then maybe that was what kept them together. Their yelling was like glue.

Perhaps I was hypnotized by Gary and his mother's banter because all along I was standing with the warm spatula in my hand but was not paying attention to the grill. I was not myself. I was in the process of becoming less and less of my former self while becoming more and more of something else I couldn't yet define. Gary's words were like heat rising from the flames of his hot breath, which he breathed into me as if he were molding me into something else—into an Adam or a golem or some magical creature that had once been a handful of dirt but was now under his spell.

Anyway, I stood there in my trance watching him dig that hole while he was half dressed as if he had fled a burning house. He must have sensed my steady gaze because at one point he stood up with one hand on his hip and stared directly at me like an animal sizing up a meal he was confident of swallowing.

I waved to him with the spatula.

Was he thinking about me as much as I was now thinking about him? It seemed impossible that it could be any other way. My consumption of who he was must have been equaled by his consumption of me, but I never considered that the word *consumption* could be so different between us. I was consumed with me becoming *him*. I didn't know then that he was consumed with me becoming *his*.

In the meantime I let the hamburgers burn down into craggy meat rocks that smoldered like pointy hunks of smoking meteorites. The hamburger buns were lacy domes of gray ash that sifted through the grill grate and down onto the flames.

Normally I would have been worried about the ruined food and my thoughtless waste of the family dinner, but instead an unusual moment of calm came over me. Fire changes everything so quickly. If I didn't care about being in trouble, then consequences had no power over me. My apathy dissolved my alarm. I used the spatula to scrape up and then catapult the charred nuggets of meat into the air. They arced about twenty feet overhead and then hit the fleshy surface of the canal like someone being slapped across the face.

That drew my mother's attention to where I was standing and she came rushing down to judge for herself what exactly I had screwed up.

When she saw, she looked furious and said, "Didn't I tell you not to ruin this?"

"Don't worry," I said before she kept at me. "I'm getting rid of the evidence before Dad notices."

"What has happened to you?" she asked, both cross and puzzled. "All you had to do was flip them back and forth like you've done a million times. It couldn't be easier."

"If you do easy stuff for too long it becomes hard," I said without emotion. "Even monkeys get tired of monkeying around."

"What's gotten into you?" she asked. "You're talking like an idiot. And is that blood on your shirt?"

I didn't have to answer because Gary suddenly shouted out, "I'm ready for the body, Mom!"

"It's about time," Mrs. Pagoda fired back as my mother looked over at their house in shock.

Then as our curiosity quietly froze us both in place, Mrs. Pagoda called for Gary's dad, who was in some inner part of the house.

"Mr. P!" she said sharply as if jabbing him awake from a nap. "Mr. Pickles. Get up offa your divan, it's time for the funeral!"

My mother gave me a nudge. "What funeral?" she whispered. "And who is Mr. Pickles?"

"I think it's a pet name for the dad," I replied, and then I pointed my nose toward the open hole. "And that would be for the dog funeral."

"Well, we don't have time for this perverse spectacle," she said impatiently. "And don't throw the meat in the canal—those awful fish will just get all overexcited and want more."

Then, from inside our house, we heard the smooth voice of Nat King Cole singing, "Mona Lisa, Mona Lisa." My sister, Karen, had turned up the stereo. It was my father's favorite song and he always sang along with it as his fancy footwork glided around our house in dance-floor circles.

Hastily my mother turned toward our back porch and frowned. "I'm sweating," she said with exasperation, and dabbed a paper napkin at the half moon of perspiration under her sleeveless blouse. "And you've ruined the meal. Let's hope your sister holds the fort."

My sister must have seen my father pull into the driveway and put the record on with the volume turned up. And now she was saving the day or, should I say, saving the trophy moment, because on the back porch, in her outstretched arms, she was holding forth a cookie sheet ready for the Commodore's inspection. On it was brilliantly modeled a birthday cake shaped after the USS *Newport News*, which was our Sea Cadet chapter's sponsor ship.

"Happy birthday, Dad," she said warmly just as he danced around the corner from the front of the house.

Then she presented him with the cake as if she were the real Mona Lisa while Nat King Cole crooned about men bringing dreams to her doorstep.

He grinned widely as he raised his arms to greet her. "Now, this is a trophy moment," he declared gleefully above the music, and grasped one end of the tray and then the two of them slid it carefully onto the patio table.

He knelt down on one knee to examine the red-tipped cannons, which were made of candy cigarettes. Then his eyes glazed over when he saw, up on the bridge of the cake ship, the standing Commodore modeled out of marzipan with a row of marzipan sailors saluting him. The smokestacks were made of curled thin sheets of licorice. Even the line of signal flags flying from the jack staff on the bow and up to the bridge flagstaff and over to the stacks and back to the stern ensign staff read HAPPY BIRTHDAY COMMODORE, exactly like the ones I had already burned. The ship sat on a dappled sea of blue icing with churning white foam rolling outward from the prop wash. My sister had thought of everything.

My mother turned the music down.

Dad beamed. He danced around the cake while murmuring, "Mona Lisa, Mona Lisa," as his eyes searched out every nautical detail. "Wonderful. Marvelous. Genius," he declared in a singsongy voice while sneaking swipes of battleship-gray icing off the ship's hull.

He had been giddy like this all my life. I never questioned it, but suddenly his cheerfulness seemed artificial, as if his life was the repetition of a recorded song going around and around, repeating itself day after day until the day came when the record got old and thin and silent and the needle peeled the vinyl into a circular curl of the Mona Lisa's silent hair. Could having a family like us really make him happy, or was this an accidental life he was trying to make the best of, which was why all his joy seemed so vastly overinflated?

He seemed like a hot-air balloon on the verge of exploding and showering us with the confetti of all the shredded dreams that had kept him going. I couldn't tell if I was being too rough on him. Yesterday he seemed the same as I had always known him. But today I couldn't be sure, and if I judged him differently, wouldn't I judge myself differently, too? How could I know he was so full of hot air unless I was, too?

"Who made this dreamboat?" he finally asked, and his eyes flashed mischievously as he snapped off the portside candy anchor and crunched down on it. "Which da Vinci of the ship's galley created this masterpiece?"

My sister had done every meticulous bit of the work. I was no help, though she had asked me to assist with painting on the ocean of icing, which was the easiest task, but I had told her I was busy.

I had been watching television. It was a show on how to repair cars. The narrator-mechanic talked like he had a mouthful of ball bearings. He had a nasty scar running up under his neck that then hooked upward over his chin and connected with the tip of a V-shaped gap in his floppy lower lip. I guessed he had stuck his head too far under the hood and got hacked a good one by the fan blade. His lower lip warbled when he spoke, but still he knew what he was talking about, and he was efficient with his hands, which did most of the teaching anyway. I liked knowing how to repair flat tires and change water pumps and spark plugs. I wanted a car and figured I'd only get a junker, so I'd need to know how to fix it up, which was why I didn't pitch in and help my sister.

Mom had promised to assist with the cake, but then she got busy with a nursery project putting up wallpaper cows jumping over grinning moons in the baby's room.

"The moon looks a little depraved," I had remarked that morning when I stuck my head around the corner. "It's smiling like Hermann Göring." I was on a kick where I tried to ruin each innocent moment by perversely listing the deeds of every evil Nazi I could recall. I was good at history.

"Don't be morbid," she replied. "The wallpaper will guard the baby against germs."

"Or Germans," I remarked as I slouched back to my car repair show. Mom continued to hang the wallpaper. My sister continued to sing to her records and create her masterpiece.

Now, as my father looked eagerly into all of our faces to learn who had constructed the ship cake, I stared down at my roughed-up shoes. I expected my sister to take the full credit she deserved.

"We all contributed," she said graciously. "It was family teamwork."

She knew that saying the word *teamwork* was like magnifying his extra-tall, extra-gilded trophy moment because the instant she said it he livened up even more and launched into one of his instructional naval discourses.

"A ship, like a family, is only as good as the teamwork of her sailors," he announced as if reading out the title of a treasured lecture he was about to deliver. Then he rattled on for a while as my mind begged to drift off toward the Pagoda animal burial.

At our cadet meetings, where we practiced tying elaborate boat knots and attempted to carve tiny sailing ships that fit into impossibly tinier bottles, my father often took the time to address us as a unit.

He would stand up on the seat of a chair and begin a talk with, "Crew, nobody likes to be a weak link on a ship. Now, boys, everyone line up side by side."

There were only about twenty of us. We groaned as we put down our half-made elaborate boat knots, which would snailishly fall open again, or sheathed our woodcarving knives, and then we all lined up about a foot apart from each other.

"Now, get close enough so that you can lock arms," Dad ordered, eyeing us impatiently.

We did. We had done it many times before, so we knew the drill by heart.

"I want the two end boys to circle around," he instructed, "and link up to form a perfect, impenetrable circular chain."

He rhythmically clapped his hands together to motivate us. Once the end boys linked arms he began to tap a beat with his foot and sing an old sea chantey that he knew we loved.

"What shall we do with a drunken sailor?" he bellowed. "What shall we do with a drunken sailor? What shall we do with a drunken sailor? Early in the morning."

Then we all sang back, "Put him in the long boat 'til he's sober. Pull out the bung and wet him all over. Heave him by the leg . . ."

By then we were singing so wildly and dancing like cows kicking our legs this way and that until one of us got lifted off his feet and tilted over and then the whole chain of us would wobble a bit and slowly collapse inward with a final slaphappy groan. Then we'd have to pull our arms free and get up and do it again.

Dad was dead set on everyone working together as a unit and conforming to the theory of the "unbreakable chain of collective strength."

"When you're under enemy fire," he instructed sagely, "every moment lost to confusion results in a casualty. It is worthy of a court-martial to waste a man's life because of poor training."

Now as Dad stood in front of the birthday cake he rubbed his half-fingered fist into the palm of his good hand. I saw that stubby finger jiggle like a tongue wagging and thought of his Jack Ruby comment from breakfast. It was a stupid joke, but then I had laughed anyway. It was a teamwork laugh, I supposed, or maybe I was just being spineless.

But suddenly the references seemed as *contemptible* as Mom had said and I no longer felt part of his team. If I had shown any guts I would have backed her up by blurting out, "I think it's a stupid joke, too." But sometimes agreeing with Mom left me the target of Dad's annoyance, and he could fume and hold a grudge for a week, so I had kept my mouth shut.

Then, from behind Dad's back, and lurking on the other side of the fence, Gary and his father appeared and were breathing heavily as they leaned forward like fishermen pulling a net full of fish. They strained to drag a large canvas tarp toward the grave. I guessed the greyhound was wrapped in the tarp.

Mom cast a puzzled glance over at the panting, struggling Pagodas and I wished she hadn't. At first I thought Mr. Pickles was wearing a large red-velvet cake on his head. As he tugged the tarp forward I realized it was a Shriners fez, and the elaborately knotted tassel swung back and forth in front of the ceremonial silver scimitar and Moorish moon like a scolding finger saying "No, no, no." For a second I thought Mom was going to invite them over for cake, but then she must have summed them up as hazardous social germs because she turned her back toward them and announced cheerfully, "Family-trophy-moment photo!"

"Indeed!" Dad agreed, and drew himself up to attention.

Mom quickly retrieved the camera with the flash cube from the kitchen and Dad stood with the cake tray tilted forward, but not too forward, and my sister and I knelt like bookends on either side of him. It was a classic trophy-moment photograph.

Then I took a photo of Mom and Karen and Dad. Then Karen took one of me and Mom and Dad. By then the mosquitoes had begun to rise up off the canal into winged formations of humming hypodermics and we carried the cake into the kitchen, where Dad did the honors of slicing it up according to Mr. Bowditch's famous nautical rules on latitude and longitude. I received a shallow piece of the ocean but didn't dare complain. I ate it while peering out the window, trying to get a better sense of what Gary and his dad were doing. But I only saw a final glimpse of Mr. Pickles pushing up on the lower edge of his fez, which had slipped down over his eyes that were as wrinkled as raw oysters. Then he adjusted the fez as if he were carefully straightening a lampshade while he trotted toward his wine-colored Cadillac. He obviously had a Shriners meeting to attend and left the rest of the work to Gary.

Since the hamburgers were ruined Dad suggested that he and Mom go to the Sea Cadet Commodores' cocktail party at the Kon-Tiki Club after all. He had been going to skip the party because of his birthday celebration, but now without dinner I had inadvertently given him and Mom an excuse to get away from us.

It didn't take them long to spruce up, and once they left the house my sister put on my mother's lipstick and came up to me and playfully punched me in the shoulder.

"I know you burned the banner," she said slyly. "You are such a clown. Now you owe me one for keeping my mouth shut. And after what you did to the burgers you owe it to yourself to start paying attention to what you are doing."

She was right, but I wasn't in a mood to be wrong. My mistakes always made me respond like a jerk.

"Yeah," I said. "Thanks. I'll pay you back when you least expect it."

"Moron," she replied in a tired voice. "You are too stupid to know when people are being nice to you."

She was always more fair to me than I was to her, and somehow this kept me from being totally honest with her. I wasn't smarter than her, so being a liar was my only way of trying to get the upper hand, but she saw right through me.

"And what were you and that kid in the skanky underwear talking about down by the canal?" she asked suspiciously. "That was pretty weird."

I shrugged. "Nothing," I said. "Just saying hi."

The less I said about him the better. As a kid I learned that when you announced you had an invisible friend it was no longer invisible. It was best to keep Gary in the shadows.

Karen continued. "And could you figure out what he and his dad were doing out back?" she asked. "They were creeping around like they were burying something illegal."

"They are burying a greyhound," I explained. "Gary was digging the hole."

"I hope it doesn't smell," she remarked.

"It's a deep hole," I added, cutting off the subject.

"Well, I'm going to visit Suzy," she said, and headed for the door. Then from over her shoulder she added, "Watch it. Suzy said that guy's a two-faced user. And she should know."

Suzy Pryor was a friend of hers from two schools ago when we lived in Lauderhill and just by coincidence she was now living in the same Wilton Manors neighborhood we had moved into. They had been thrilled to discover each other again and were already planning out what activities they wanted to get involved with once school started. They were the type of girls who lived to organize clubs and run for class office. They were smart and energetic and had each other.

This would be my sixth new school in eight grades. I wasn't looking forward to another friendless year all over again. I guess you could say I didn't make real friends. I just hung around groups of kids and mimed being a friend. I'd silently laugh at their jokes, but I might just as well have been laughing into a mirror because I was the only one watching me.

I hadn't made any plans for school other than to show up on time and keep my mouth shut. In my last school I had been in the Latin club and the chess club. Maybe I'd do that again. They were easy clubs to join because they had so few members they didn't even reject the rejects. If you hung around enough you got your picture in the yearbook and pretended to be a part of something. I did. In the chess club photo I had stood with my arms high across my chest and head tilted forward in a pose that I thought would make me appear moody and troubled—as if I were someone artistically conflicted that you'd want to know. But when I saw the photo my pug face made me look like I was too mentally dim to speak Latin or play chess—and no one sought me out to get to know me better. I looked like the IQ equal of our pathetic club mascot—a three-foot-high brown Naugahyde pawn with a metal ruler stabbed into its ball-peen head and a flag taped to the ruler that read RULE THE WORLD ONE MOVE AT A TIME.

I wished the expressions on my face matched up to my thoughts, but they rarely did. Only when I was in extreme physical pain did my face knot up and truly express extreme physical pain. Happiness looked like a square peg struggling to fit into a round hole. It was all mismatched. When it came to my heart I felt everything okay, but when I tried to express my feelings the words came out of me like invisible ink.

Before Karen left the house I said, "Tell Suzy I very much look forward to seeing her."

I purposely spoke in a big, proper sentence because I had a crush on Suzy that had suddenly revived when I fantasized how she might possibly pull up in front of our house and rescue me in a white pickup truck and give me that flaming-hot kiss I wanted.

Karen stopped with her hand on the doorknob. "Let me give you some girlfriend advice," she said, turning toward me. "You should pay more attention to girls whose Salvation Army missionary work is trying to save tragic boys like you. Being a reclamation project is the only chance you have of attracting a girl as immature as you are."

"I'm *not* immature," I said defensively.

"Remember the burning flags today? The ruined food? Your infatuation with your new half-naked skinny-legged friend? Remember that weighing the pros and cons of the world around you is a sign of maturity."

"I got bored," I said. "Most of life is boring. It's only what I'm thinking about between the boring parts that keeps me from killing myself." This was true only because I wished it to be true.

"Please don't share any more of your perpetually self-involved thoughts," she said. "Just clean up the kitchen and the outside mess so Mom doesn't make herself sick tomorrow by trying to disinfect the entire backyard with something that could hurt the baby. You know how obsessive she gets when it comes to germs."

"Germans," I mumbled.

She then went up the street to see Suzy. My eyes followed her until I imagined myself knocking on Suzy's door.

DEPTH CHARGE

After I cleaned the kitchen that evening I was thinking about Gary and the dog burial, so I opened the back door and stepped outside.

To the west the bright eyelashes of the sun garishly stretched across the sky for one final cameo, while to the east the pebbly clouds glowed like orange peels beneath those copper rays.

I balanced myself on Chief Osceola and watched the distant horizon until the blazing rind of the sun set with a final flash of green light. The sky turned gray as darkness rose from the ground like a creeping tide. Sounds became softer. Air became cooler.

I flicked on the yard lights and walked down toward the warm grill and dragged it over to its usual place by the Pagoda fence. Gary had returned and was still working. He was on his hands and knees and grunting with animal effort as he hard-packed the sandy dirt down on the grave with overhead strokes of the flat back of a shovel. A black standard poodle sat in the shade of a palm tree watching him work.

"Is that you?" he asked, without turning toward me.

"Yes. Did you bury the greyhound?"

"It was only a Chinese crested," he replied. "But it had the guts of a greyhound. Pound for pound, nobody packed more bark and bite in a body than little Baby Chairman Mao."

"It seemed a lot bigger than a Chinese crested," I remarked. "It looked to me like you and your dad were dragging something heavy, like the size of a Great Dane."

Gary stood and carefully brushed the damp sand off his knees. Then he turned toward me as he locked his arms across the front of his unzipped jacket. His knuckles looked like a row of saddles linked across the scarred tops of his wide fists.

"I like you," he said in a deliberately cold and emotionless tone. His white face could just as easily have been a coral head with eyes and a mouth scratched on it. "And I was just thinking today that we might even become good friends, but now when you question what I tell you it makes me think you don't know the correct rules on how to be my friend."

That caught me by surprise. I thought we had just been very friendly, even friendlike, and the dog comment wasn't offensive. But maybe I was trying to be a friend too quickly, which was against his rules.

"I'm sorry," I replied, and stepped back a pace. "I didn't realize a Chinese crested could be so big."

"Well, now you know the facts," he said with clipped authority. "So when I say something *is* what it *is* you don't have to question it—just take my word for it, especially when it comes to dogs, because I train them at the track, my sister grooms them, my mom's kind of a vet, and my dad bets on them. So we *know* dogs."

From moving around so much with my family I had learned it was better to let strangers take the upper hand and say whatever they felt like saying—that way I could custom-fit my jigsawed answers to what they wanted to hear.

Most people liked people who agreed with them and I wanted to be liked, especially by Gary. I never had a friend like him and I could feel the panic in my gut that I had crossed him.

"How'd Chairman Mao die?" I asked, sounding more sympathetic than I was feeling.

"Rabies. We had to put him down. Chihuahua nipped his hind leg in the first round of a fight," he replied. "Some of the dog owners don't pay to inoculate their street dogs. I guess they figure they won't live long enough to get rabies—but this one must have. Either that, or my sister bit him."

"I have a sister, too," I said, trying to shift the conversation to common ground.

"I already checked her out," he replied without fanfare. "Not my type. One look and I could tell she's the kind of girl who wants to improve guys."

"You got that right," I said.

"I prefer girls who let guys improve them," he continued.

"I think I could improve some girls," I ventured.

He looked up at me for a moment and finally smiled at something I said.

"Are you the kind of guy who tries to pick up girls in study hall by helping them with their math homework?"

"English homework," I said uneasily, hesitant to correct him, but to be honest, I was lousy at math. "I like to help, and girls like smart guys—especially book guys."

"Did you see that girl in the white truck the other day?" he asked. He must have seen me watching. "Well, she doesn't drive a pickup for nothing. She drove down here from Alabama to have a little phys-ed study hall with me."

"Alabama?" I repeated. "How'd you meet her?"

"She's my girlfriend. Leigh Dupont. Used to live in *your* house," he said. "In your room," he added pointedly, "and I could reach right through the window and touch her."

That's where my bed was.

"But her family moved up there from here." He adjusted the sagging waistband of his undershorts and spit to one side, then added, "To get her away from me after *some jilted neighbor told them a shitload of lies about me.*" He was speaking loudly while looking at the fenced-in house on the other side of ours, as if he wanted whoever lived there to hear him.

I didn't say anything to that other than to privately imagine Leigh Dupont in my room, reaching out toward me with both her slender arms.

"That's how I ended up back in juvie this spring," he continued. "I wired a car and went up to see her and got popped."

"Too bad," I said.

"Not really," he replied, and looked up at the stars. "An hour with her was worth a stretch in juvie."

I was going to agree with him, but then I didn't know what a month in juvie meant or what an hour with a girl really meant besides trying to help one write complete sentences for a book report.

"I saw that your dad drives a Rambler—you got an extra key?" he asked. "Or does that piece of junk even need a key—maybe you just kick it in the ass in the morning and it farts right up?"

I wished Gary would hot-wire Dad's Rambler and take it away for good. It was embarrassing to be seen in it. Dad now worked as a traveling salesman for a concrete firm and his new company car had a gray-and-tan concrete I-beam logo with CUSTOM CONCRETE painted down both sides along with a bright red phone number. Still, I was afraid to give Gary the key.

"If you get me the key I could make a copy so he wouldn't think you did it," he suggested slyly. "I'd be doing him a favor if that piece of crap ended up burned and dumped in the Everglades."

"Yeah," I said. "But it's the only car we have and my mom's pregnant, and he travels for work . . ."

He sighed impatiently. "Then I'll return it without one little itsy-bitsy scratch," he said. "He'd never know a thing. I'd drive up at night. See my girl. Have some fun. Drive back here before your dad wakes up."

"Doesn't it take about ten hours just to drive up to Alabama?" I asked, knowing it did.

"Not the way I drive," he said. "I used to race cars. Mini-roadsters on dirt tracks. I got a room full of trophies. You should see them someday."

"Yeah, I'd like to," I said, and was still nervous he was going to ask about my dad's car key again.

"Maybe we could take turns driving the Rambler," he suggested. "And I could give you some professional racing tips on how to outwit the cops."

I didn't even have my learner's permit yet.

Then as I hesitated he suddenly shifted gears. "Hey, my dad's gone, my mom's dead asleep, and your parents are out. Let's have a pool party." He clapped his hands together and smiled.

There was no fighting that wide smile. It was like a double broadside of cannons turning toward your starboard side, and just as convincing.

"Sure," I replied eagerly—anything to get away from the car talk.

"I know a great game," he said with enthusiasm. "They should add it to the Tokyo Olympics. I'm always inventing the Pagoda Olympic Games of the Future, and this one is called Tojo Depth Charge. I've been thinking about it all afternoon—that fire you started whetted my appetite for a little mayhem."

"I'm good with fire," I said with confidence.

"As far as I know it's your best quality," he confirmed. "You were like Thor at his forge over there. That grill fire was so hot I thought you were going to mold that steel spatula into a Viking branding iron and use it to burn a war oath to Odin on yourself."

I grinned. "Yeah," I said. "I thought about it."

"What part of the body?" he asked.

"Undecided," I said, because it seemed better to be vague.

"Remember, tender skin scars the brightest," he advised, "like the neck, or the inside of the thigh, or higher up. But for now come over in fifteen minutes. Get your swim trunks on. I'll tell my little brother, Frankie, to get ready, too. You'll like him. I call him 'the Cross and the Switchblade' because he carves all the fancy little dog coffins and crosses for our pet cemetery. My sister's home, but she's doing a leopard-spot color treatment and perm job on a poodle tonight. We have a pet grooming business in the garage. Mostly we just do celebrity pets. This poodle belongs to the owner of Big Daddy's Liquors." He pointed over his shoulder to his garage. "If you want," he said, "she can cut your hair to make you look like a celebrity ferret. She's a pro."

"Does she do yours?"

"I do it myself," he said. "Without a mirror. Comes out different each time. Girls *love* inconsistency—keeps 'em guessin'."

"Yeah," I said, running my hand over my taut cadet hair like I was petting a bottle brush. "I need a cut."

"I'll fix you up with my sister," he insisted. "She'll make you look more like Sailor Jerry instead of that Junior Popeye hair you got now—that is, unless you want all your girlfriends to look like Olive Oyl."

"Who's Sailor Jerry?" I asked.

"Greatest tattoo artist in the world," he replied. "I'm saving up to have my whole back done in a 'Love Thy Neighbor' design—it's a skull made out of a straight razor, brass knuckles, and a blackjack, all dripping in blood."

"Wow," I said.

"I'll come up with one for you, too," he said. "I think your gang name should be Flame-Out, so I'll work that into a design. But let's get going."

I quickly turned and went into the house to rustle up a swimsuit. "Flame-Out," I whispered to myself. "A gang name." I liked it, though I couldn't picture in my mind what a flame-out looked like. Was I a jet that had suffered an engine flame-out and crashed? Or was I a jet that had suffered a flame-out and survived through superior piloting? It was impossible to tell what Gary was imagining. Death seemed as exhilarating as life to him.

In my room I had a bathing suit, but my mother had bought it for me at a thrift store and it was a bright pink-and-white lobster print with loopy rope piping along the edges and outlined lobster-claw pockets on either side. It did not look like anything Sailor Jerry would tattoo on a real man or a dead man or even a boy. It looked like something only a mother would buy for a son to keep him from becoming a real man.

I quickly took a pair of scissors out of the kitchen drawer and went into my bedroom. I pulled out some old Levi's, cut the legs off them just above the knees, stripped off my cadet uniform, and put them on. Then I had a clever idea. I got my lobster suit and ripped the rope piping off, ran it through my belt loops, and tied the ends in a square knot like a pirate belt. I looked into the mirror. The suit was okay, but I looked so small. I played no sports. I didn't work out. I had the milky physique of a very soft boy.

Why would Gary ever choose me as a friend? He was built like a boxer. He must have had friends who looked more like him. I was like some boneless squid. I turned away from the mirror. It was discouraging to look at myself. My STP T-shirt was in the wash, so I put my cadet shirt back on.

A few minutes later I headed out. I hopped the chain-link fence and landed on the freshly packed dirt but didn't waste time wondering why Gary had dug such a deep grave for such a small dog because I didn't believe him anyway. As I stood on the grave it gave me an odd sense of power that he had lied to hide something from me. If I knew the truth it would be more powerful than his lie—though what good would the truth do me? Like my dad, Gary always had the last word.

I shrugged and let that thought fade as I walked over to the pool where Gary was pouring fuel from a red metal gas can into a plastic mop bucket. He was dressed exactly the same as before. I figured he'd swim, sleep, shower, and eat in the same outfit.

"Is that gasoline?" I asked, sniffing.

"Diesel," he replied. "Germans chug a shot for breakfast and it keeps them regular all day long."

His younger brother opened the back kitchen door and waddled out onto the patio like a seal. He was eating a pimento cheese sandwich and wearing a full-body black rubber wetsuit and swim fins. He had a diver's mask propped up on his forehead with a double-long snorkel fixed to the side of the mask.

"I'm Jack," I said, and stuck out my hand to shake. He looked at my hand and violently shoved the remainder of the sandwich in his mouth as if he were suddenly plugging a leaky boat.

"Is that all you're wearing?" he mumbled with his mouth full, and reached down to adjust the straps on his fins while looking me over. Then he stuck his finger deep into his mouth and wiggled it around to unclog his throat.

"Why?" I replied.

He turned toward Gary and swallowed hard. "Did you tell him how to play this game?" he asked. "Because if he gets harpooned like Eddie the Whale when we played Olympic Moby-Dick, I don't want to be arrested."

Gary shrugged. "Fair enough," he said. "Here is the short description of the game."

He bent over and lowered the can of diesel fuel and began to screw the cap back onto the spout.

"First I pour the plastic bucket of fuel on the pool and then give it a few minutes until it's pretty much evenly spread over the surface of the water. Once I set it on fire," he explained as he pointed toward the diving board, "then I turn off the pool light and go stand at the tip of the board, where you can now see that I already have that half box of twelve M-80s. You two Japanese mini-submarines dive into the water, and then I count to ten with my eyes closed and when I open them I light the fuse on an M-80 and throw it in such a way that it lands just above you and blows you out of the water and you surrender—end of game."

I was trying not to look afraid. The M-80 was the most powerful firecracker in the world. It would blow mailboxes to smithereens. Watermelons were turned into red rain. It was like a suburban hand grenade. There was no doubt that it could blow the top of your head off.

Frankie must have seen the fear on my face. "There's a trick to the whole thing," he said casually. "Just stay belly-down on the bottom like a gator. The fuses are short and they blow up before they can sink down and get close to you."

"He's right," Gary agreed. "Just hug the bottom."

"What do you do about breathing?" I asked, trying to sound practical.

"I have my adjustable snorkel," Frankie said, and shrugged. "And a tennis racket."

"I don't," I replied, and turned toward Gary.

"A snorkel is for sissies," Gary said derisively, and flashed his eyes at Frankie. "It just gets in the way of the strategy."

"What strategy?" I asked, eager for some survival tips.

"Well," he said, "let's say I throw a lit M-80 at you when you surface to breathe—right away you have two options. Either you can dive for your life, or you can show some manhood and catch the M-80 in one hand and wing it back at me and hope to blow my face off and win the game."

I looked over at Frankie. He was getting impatient. He kept adjusting all his gear and fidgeting with this and that. Finally he blurted out, "No one yet has gone for the option of catching the M-80 because if it goes off in your hand they'll soon be calling you Captain Hook. So I've now included the tennis racket."

Gary lunged forward and yanked the tennis racket from Frankie's hand.

"Cheater," he sneered, and threw the racket toward the canal. "I don't like people who can't play by the Pagoda Olympics rules."

"But the racket gives me a safer option," Frankie whined. "I can just swat it back at you."

"We have *already* agreed to the established options," Gary insisted, like a TV lawyer, "and there will be no deviations." Gary then turned toward me. "Now, since you are the guest, Sailor Jack, you have the honor of kicking off the game."

Right away I liked being called Sailor Jack. It sounded cooler than Flame-Out and I figured a second nickname meant he already thought of me as a friend.

It was a warm feeling that passed through me, and another feeling, too, one even better, was that Gary already preferred me over his own brother. I'd have to keep an eye on Frankie, I thought, to make sure he didn't give away my hiding spots.

"Sailor Jack, you did a masterful job starting the grill, so you should enjoy this," Gary said, and handed me a pack of matches. "I think the diesel has spread around good enough by now. Toss a match over the pool."

I struck a match and flicked it toward the pool as if I were lighting the Olympic torch. *Flame on!* I thought to myself.

As soon as the match hit the surface a choppy crown of lime-green flames shot up and rapidly spread in an ever-growing circle until nearly all the pool's surface was on fire. An acrid black smoke swirled above the flames. I began to cough. It smelled like burning car tires.

"Turn off the pool light," Gary instructed Frankie, then scuffed in his white fake-alligator loafers toward the diving board. Frankie flipped the switch and the backyard darkened except for the pool, which was magical with the green flames swaying back and forth like waltzing doll dresses.

"Let's go," Frankie said, and dove in first, without much splash, like a stealthy seal.

I unbuttoned my shirt and tossed it on a plastic chair, then I took the deepest breath I could and jumped in with my eyes closed. I touched the bottom with my hand, righted myself, and then swam underwater toward the deep end. I felt around for the drain, found it, and anchored myself to it with my fingers. Before the first explosion I was actually enjoying how beautiful it was to look straight up at the bottom side of the flames on the water. I had only seen fire from above and was always tensed up as the flames angrily knifed at the air with their sharp blades. But when looked at from below, the flames stood up like small sails as the wind glided them across the glassy surface of the water.

It was musical to watch them until the first muffled explosion of an M-80 detonated and a rolling shock wave traveled through the water. When it reached me the pressure in my ears was painful, like a hand-slap against the sides of my head, and I instantly pushed off the bottom and went straight up. I broke the surface and took a deep breath and worked my jaw around to pop my ears, then dove over like a seal back down toward the drain. A blast went off close to the bottom of my feet and a pulsing ring of water elevated me like I was a sea offering on the palm of Neptune's hand. I turned over onto my back and slowly floated to the surface, where my lips parted the oily water between the flames, which had lessened and were now spread out like a field of blazing campfires. I breathed quietly as I watched Gary. He had his eye on Frankie's snorkel, which cut through the surface of the shallow water like a shark's fin. Gary lit one M-80, then another. He threw the first one in front of the snorkel and the second behind it. The explosions sent a lime plume of flaming water ten feet into the air. Frankie didn't surface. Dogs began to bark inside the Pagodas' garage.

"What the . . . ?" someone said from a lawn across the canal, his words carried on the breeze.

"They're doin' it again!" came a second voice that was neither a man's nor a woman's—it was something mechanical, as if it were the voice cranked out of a rusty windup toy. Then I realized it came from one of those throat devices some old ex-smokers press against a flabby gray hole in their neck after having surgery to cut out their cancerous larynx.

I hugged my knees and half exhaled as I descended toward the drain. Once I touched it, I drifted upward very slowly, inch by inch, like a bubble of tumbling air toward the flaming surface just beneath the diving board.

Gary was pacing above me. The horseshoe cleats on the heels of his shoes gouged white shavings from the fiberglass diving board. He shifted to the left, then stepped to the tip. The board creaked as it dipped downward. He was after Frankie, not me. After all, I was a new friend in training, kind of a pet. He might make me fear him, but he wouldn't hurt me. Not yet, anyway.

From the main boulevard a police siren was growing louder as it closed in on the Pagoda address. Frankie stood up in the shallow end and splashed a circle of flames away from himself.

"Time out!" he shouted. "Those old throat-croakers must have called the cops again." He pushed his mask up on top of his head. "Assholes!" he yelled loudly in the direction of the people who had complained. "Go smoke a butt and relax!"

Gary looked down to his right, where I happened to be looking straight up at him and breathing through my mouth. He could have lit the fuse of the M-80 in his hand and dropped it straight down my throat and I would have had my larynx blown out my neck.

Instead, he winked at me and struck a match. "What the hell," he muttered. "You only live once—so you better kill as many as you can."

He lit the fuse and side-armed the M-80 at Frankie, who by then had halfway pulled himself over the far edge of the pool. The M-80 clipped him across the back and caromed over the fence, where it blew up over our yard.

"Hey!" Frankie squealed as he stood up. "No fair! Truce. The police are coming and we gotta save a few for them."

With his swim fins still on he slapped across the patio like an upright frog and opened a plastic pool shed door and yanked out a fire extinguisher. Obviously he had done this before. He flipped it upside down and pulled the pin, and when he squeezed the trigger it seemed as if an entire tanker truck of whipped cream sprayed out of the wide nozzle. I hopped out of the pool and put my shirt on as he squatted down and slowly circled the pool until he had layered a thick blanket of fire-retardant foam over the entire surface.

For a moment, beneath the foam, the still-burning diesel transformed the pool into a fancy flaming dessert with the Key-lime-green flames flickering upward and peeking deliciously through the singed milky tips of the whipped cream. But slowly the retardant worked and the flames dimmed and fizzled out and the putrid diesel fumes wafted up like toxic smoke rings.

I pulled my shirt collar across my mouth and breathed. The smell burned my throat. It worried me. I didn't want to someday speak through a mechanical larynx.

The siren on the cop car wound down.

"Battle stations," Gary ordered. "Frankie, take the ammo and hide it in the garage and play like you've been helping Alice with the dog perm. Sailor Jack—hit the fence and disappear. I'll do all the talking since I probably know them anyway."

I hopped the fence but didn't go inside. There were so many possible lives to lead, but hiding from my fear wasn't one of them. I didn't want to sit in the house and watch TV and play like I was innocent. I wanted to get a close-up view of the danger. I was breathing hard when I pressed my chest against one of our palm trees and tried to catch a glimpse of the police. I didn't think they'd be looking for me. If they knew Gary so well maybe they'd walk right into his house and escort him out in handcuffs.

There was only a single cop and he looked out his cruiser window and slowly scanned the sidewalks as he rolled down our street. Once he passed our house I took a chance and dashed into the front yard and flattened myself against the dark side of a palm tree. Slowly the cruiser circled the cul-de-sac, and when the cop turned off the engine the car kept rolling until inertia brought the sticky tires to a final stop directly across from the Pagoda house.

Without warning the cop flicked a switch and turned on his door-mounted spotlight. The beam had a canary-yellow cast to it, like the color of shame. It strangely bleached the pigment from whatever it passed over, as if to disgrace it.

The cop trained the manual spotlight's bright circle on the Pagoda front door, then slowly he shifted the light over to the picture window so he could see deeper into the house interior. A boxy square reflection of one of the Pagodas' wall mirrors blinked directly back at the cop and lit up his startled expression. When nothing of value came of that window scan he ran the light slowly over the low shrubs around the house foundation. A bush moved and he held the spotlight steady, but maybe it was just one of the Korean snakehead fish flopping around like a detached foot. The beam inched up the drain spout and then methodically scanned back and forth across the roof. If the light were a pencil eraser the house would have vanished.

Then the cop flicked a switch and the light turned off. The car engine ticked with escaping heat.

Wherever Gary and Frankie and Alice were hiding they didn't reveal themselves. The windshield of the cruiser faced me. The single cop sat hatless and lit a cigarette. In a while he peeled the cellophane off a box of candy, tilted his head back and shook some into his mouth. I could hear the hard candy click against his teeth. His police radio squawked and he turned it off. It must have reminded him of his other radio, so he turned it on and I could hear the jingle for WFUN and then Elvis sang "Crying in the Chapel." The cop sang falsetto over the backup harmonies. He was pretty good.

I felt the rough outer fibers of the crusty palm bark against my cheek. When I scuffed my skin against the trunk it smelled like the dried spices my mother kept in a kitchen drawer. Maybe it was coriander I was thinking of, or cardamom. Then it came to me that it smelled faintly of the sandalwood incense my sister burned in her room with the lights turned low as she listened to her records. The sandalwood smoke and music drifted out from under her door and turned the hallway into a waiting room where I sometimes quietly leaned against her doorjamb and hoped to receive an invitation to enter. But I always knew I was excluded.

Once I had broken down and knocked. When she answered I asked to join her.

"I won't say a word," I promised, "or sing. I'll sit by the wall on the dark side of the bed. You won't know I'm there. I really just need to get away from myself."

My voice was reedy from whispering and begging at the same time.

"Sorry," she said, and softly touched my shoulder.

For a minute she let her hand rest there like a firm and empathetic bridge between us. I realized that's all

I needed—just a reassuring touch to steady me as I sorted out my own thoughts.

Finally she said, “It takes privacy to find your true self.” She patted my shoulder. “That’s why I like to be alone. And you have to learn to be alone, too.”

I had grown up shadowing her from room to room. I was restless without her. I feared being alone. She’d tolerate me when I was younger, but even then it was a rule that I had to remain silent. Lately she hadn’t tolerated me all that much. But for some reason this one time it seemed like she was the one who needed to talk and I was eager to listen.

“What do you mean?” I asked, trying to draw her out.

“Once I was the most beautiful baby girl in the world,” she said in a weird fairy-tale whisper. “And I was chosen to be born into our family.” Then with some creeping sadness in her voice she continued. “Over time that baby grew up and slowly transformed into the misshapen girl I am now. I’m like a cliffside tree with branches desperately reaching to run away with the wind. I can’t get out of here fast enough. I’ve grown up to become a grotesque version of that beautiful baby girl. How could that happen?”

I knew what she was talking about because when I was young I was exactly who I said I was, and did what

I thought was right to do. Then as I got older I left that true self behind and began to know myself only through the eyes of the people around me. I reshaped myself and made it easier for everyone to think I was doing okay because I learned to do just okay things. But I wasn't okay. I was lost. Still, I loved the word *okay*. It was a magic word that cast a paralyzing spell over my parents while I was busy searching to become the opposite of okay.

Something like that must have happened to my sister, too, though I never noticed because I was always thinking about myself. Now I wished I had paid more attention to her.

"I wish," she continued, turning back to herself, "that there was a path of words I could walk down and they would lead me into a grotto pool where I could re-purify myself and return to the girl I was. But there isn't a path, or even a girl. She's gone, and I'm stuck trying to invent who I want to be, and I'm finding that figuring out who I want to be is so much harder than just being who I was when I was a little kid."

On that happy thought she lowered her hand from my shoulder. "You'll see," she said. "Everyone foolishly goes through hating their past—when they should realize it is the one true thing you have." Then she retreated to her room, closed the door, and turned up her stereo.

Now, with my face scuffed up against the palm trunk, I was beginning to understand what she meant. The questions that troubled her were mine, too—they were the questions of people who didn't have faith in themselves. But how we built faith in ourselves was different. She wanted to rearrange her past and bring truth and purity back into her future. But I wanted to invent my future any way I could, and being a better liar was a better path. When I looked into the mirror I wanted to see a lot less of me and a lot more of some invented kid—Gary's kind of kid. That's the faith I wanted.

Suddenly I had a temptation to do something bad to that cop. But what? What would Gary do? Let the air out of the cop's tires? Or throw a rock at the windshield? That seemed too stupid. Yet the desire to do whatever Gary might do was a growing thunderhead above me and I just wished I could be struck by the lightning of a great idea.

Then what I never imagined might happen, did happen. Gary walked out his front door and with his metal horseshoe cleats on his heels kicking up sparks across the asphalt he slowly sauntered up to the cop's open window. He said something and there was a chuckle and they shook hands. Gary then walked around the front of the car and got into the front passenger seat. He took a cigarette from a pack the cop offered, then lit it and blew smoke sideways out the window.

They sat there, talking casually. I could hear the brighter sounds of laughter and above the car's roofline I could see Gary's hand quickly waving back and forth, flopping like a glove. Maybe it was just a gesture for something he was saying, but it looked more like a "hurry-up" hand signal. Then he lowered his hand and from a corner of my eye I saw the arc of a sparkling fuse. Frankie must have tied the remaining M-80s together and tossed them from behind the hedge of the other neighbors' house. They hit the thin metal roof of the squad car, bounced down onto the hood, and in an instant the soft air hardened with a booming explosion followed by the smaller pulsing explosions that echoed as they scattered down the streets. I dropped and flattened out on the lawn and gritted my teeth to remain silent.

I stayed that way, smelling the thinning cloud of flinty gunpowder while pinned down by the thousands of sun-curled grass needles that had worked their way like cat claws through my clothes and into my naked skin.

WHITE FIRE

After the M-80s had exploded on the hood of the cop car Gary kicked open his door and staggered out. He rubbed his ears and then cupped his hands around his mouth.

"Hey, Flame-Out!" he hollered. "You shouldn't have done that. I think I'm deaf, you little prick!"

As soon as he said "Flame-Out" my heart froze. He was turning me in! I was Flame-Out.

It was as if he had given me that name in order to set me up when it was his idiot brother, Frankie, who had thrown the M-80s. But Frankie was long gone and there I was, pinned to the ground just waiting for that cop to walk over and seize me by the hair and rip me clean off this wiry grass as if he were shucking the dried husk off one of the shriveled coconuts.

"Who's Flame-Out?" I heard the cop ask as he stepped out of his cruiser to walk off the blast.

"Some goofy kid," Gary replied. "The only thing I know about him is his stupid comic-book nickname and red hair."

Then he waved his hand in the opposite direction of our house. "He lives in one of those new custom homes."

The cop nodded, then quickly doubled back to his cruiser, got in and slammed the door, and took off with his red lights flashing.

Gary stood there in the dark for a moment, sniffing the air as if he were a dog sniffing me out. When he seemed to catch wind of me he trained his eyes in my direction. But I didn't leave my hiding place. I was too upset with myself to face him. I had doubted him and now I feared him.

"Good night, Sailor Jack," he said casually, and as he dragged his heels across the asphalt I thought, *Only when I become him will I overcome my fear of him.*

After he went inside I stayed chest-down on the grass carpet of claws. I wanted to feel that needling pain because it matched the pain in my heart. I deserved to suffer and my doubt was like a weight twisting my chest back and forth against the blades of grass. Later I heard the squealing bearing in the Rambler's water pump as my parents pulled up the driveway. I held my breath. I heard their low voices and the front door open and close. They never checked my bedroom. I lowered the side of my face onto my forearm and must have fallen asleep because when I woke the eastern sky was a yellowing smudge.

Inch by inch I painfully levered myself up from the bent claws of clinging grass and scooted into my house. I crept down the hall to the bathroom and quietly locked the door. I carefully unbuttoned my blood-speckled cadet shirt, but even with the buttons undone the shirt didn't drop. The needles of grass had pinned it into my chest when I threw myself down on the yard and pressed down even more forcefully. The shirt was tightly fixed to my chest by both the grass and the dried clots of blood.

I opened the medicine cabinet and took out a pair of scissors. I snipped a line up the side seam of the shirt to my underarm and then out to the lower edge of my half-sleeve. Then I snipped from the top edge of my sleeve to my collar. The back of my shirt swung open and just hung there, so I quickly cut through the opposite side seams in the same way. The whole back of the shirt dropped to the floor, but the front was still pinned and plastered to my chest. I knew it wasn't going to come off easily.

I took a deep breath and with my thumbnail and a fingernail tried to grip the head of one of the embedded grass needles, but my nails were too short to hold on. I opened the medicine cabinet again and found an old pair of fingernail clippers. The sharp, pointy bite on the curved blades would do it.

When I pinched the grass head with the clippers and extracted the first quill from my chest I made a low hissing sound like steam. That was shameful. I didn't like to feel pain, but I didn't like to show it either. Gary wouldn't. He would probably just flex his chest muscles and propel the prickers out of his body. But not me. I bit down on my lip and quietly extracted another.

It felt very satisfying to methodically pull each dry blade of grass out and line them up on the porcelain edge of the sink. It was even more satisfying to work like a surgeon in absolute silence. I had always respected the strength of silence. Whenever I picked up a smooth river rock with my hand I held it to my ear. The silence within it was as vast as the universe. In time it would erode and slowly its drifting particles would fan through the atmosphere and silently cast their pinprick shadows onto the earth.

Or, if I saw something lost, like a Kennedy half-dollar that had rolled unseen through the bars of a sewer grate, I imagined myself as that dead president whose silver lips were perpetually sealed, thus keeping his silence forever more noble than his final gasp.

Then a new image occurred to me. I pictured myself standing in the middle of a flat field of hard-packed clay. I saw myself as a nail that someone would hold point-down against a board while with their other hand they would raise a hammer and pound, pound, pound me into the wood until you could see nothing of me but my flattened head flush with the top of the board and there I'd be, inside the wood, imprisoned, mum, serenely unthinking, and just as pure white and compressed as a stick of chalk.

I kept thinking about being the tranquil nail inside that board as I silently pulled out each painfully brittle quill of grass from my chest. Along the edge of the white sink those tan quills lined up like the thin, bloody teeth of the Korean snakehead fish in our canal.

After the last quill was out, the front of the shirt still did not drop to the floor but remained pressed against my chest as if it were an adhesive blood-and-cloth scab patched across an open cavity.

I knew my next step would test the strength of my silence. I reached my right hand across to my left hip and picked at the corner of the fabric until a small flap of the shirt was free enough to grip. I tugged up a little more cloth so I could wrap the corner around my fist and then in one mechanical motion I coiled my torso downward toward that hip.

I must have looked like a discus thrower tucking into position. I could feel the muscles quivering down my back as I took a deep breath. With my grip on the shirt corner I unleashed the full torque of my upper body and in one twisting motion ripped that crusty red flag of pain clean off the small white patch of my chest.

Instantly I hunched over and again bit down on my fist. And then I bit even harder. But I succeeded. Not one sound came from my mouth.

After a few deep breaths I straightened up and felt even stronger. I soaked a towel with rubbing alcohol and scrubbed my sticky chest until the alcohol seeped into each thin wound like the cleansing tongue of a flame. I closed my eyes and mutely tensed all my muscles until the pain faded away or I got used to it.

Either way I felt I earned a trophy moment of self-control. If I ever wanted to be like Gary I had to learn that the language of pain was silence.

On my way back to my room my sister opened her bedroom door. I quickly held my bloody shirt to my chest.

"What were you doing in the bathroom for so long?" she asked, and reached out and snatched the shirt from my hands.

She stared at my chest. "Did you do this to yourself?" she whispered harshly.

I nodded. I didn't want to wake my parents.

"To yourself?" she asked again.

I nodded.

"Well, you better look in the mirror," she advised. "And I don't mean the *mirror* in the bathroom. Whatever you are doing to yourself is wrong, and if you are doing this because of Gary, then I'm warning you that you'll become as sick as he is."

I remained silent and pushed past her. I was *sick* of being myself. Talking about what I wanted would never get me what I wanted. I quickly slipped into my bedroom and locked the door.

I had been thinking that all my memories were a loud noise holding me back from my great future with Gary. That had to stop. If silence made me empty inside, then Gary's words would fill me. That made sense, so I gathered up my class notebooks and all the school projects and photographs and teacher notes and class awards and childish drawings and art collages that I had saved as if they were the essential bits of reflective squares that blazed around inside my mind like a spinning mirror ball lighting up my entire childish past. All that early work was eager to define me, to tag along like a pathetically babyish younger twin, but it all had to go because it wasn't invited where I was going. Every piece of my past was a betrayal because it was about the kid I no longer was.

I moved quickly. I filled up a pillowcase with all my stuff, and with that pillowcase over my shoulder, I went into the garage and got another can of lighter fluid and marched to the backyard. I dumped some of my things out onto the ashes of the last grill fire. Then I reached into that pillowcase and pulled out all my personal journals—they had to be the corpses on the top of the funeral pyre. They had to burn first. I hadn't written much in them, but I knew what I had written was true, which was why I feared them. They were a plea to remain as I was, to be myself and trust the fire of my own voice, but all I wanted to do was escape myself.

I flipped open the hand-sized front cover on one of my black writing books and saw my signature in fountain-pen script on the inside. A teacher once told me your own name written with your own hand is an engraved portrait, and in that ink script my name locked letters like a fortress gate that had been hammered out of wrought iron. Inside the journal each scribbled letter and word on the paper was louder and stronger than these new thoughts reshaping me into Gary's double.

I knew if I read deeper into the journals I would never escape my old self. My written words held truths about me that I didn't want to hear. Those journal sentences were stacked up like old stone fences, word upon word, from hand to pen, from the top of the page to the bottom. There was no getting around those heavily written words that came straight from my heart and were unpassable to any stranger. And I knew that if I read one sentence of my journal it would tell me to be true to myself—it would beg me to be my own man and it would turn me away from Gary and buck me off his train. But I had lost faith in myself, and without faith I hadn't the courage to reach out and turn the journal page and read beyond my fancied-up name on the endpaper.

Quickly I began to spray the pages with the oily lighter fluid. I didn't start out to hate myself, but I couldn't burn those pages unless I worked myself into a frenzy of circling around the grill and squirting more and more fire-starter onto the paper, which soaked it up as I soaked up the suspense of my own destruction. This was the only way I knew how to give up on myself, and with a lighted match held like a pen in my hand I stabbed the paper and my name disappeared. *Poof!*

The small front door of my journal burst into flames. The curling pages went up like witches' skirts burning at the stake with their twitchy madhouse laughter, but soon the flames robbed their chatter of oxygen and choked them down to a crackle. The white pages of paper flags waved their surrender to the blaze, but the merciless flames took no prisoners and blackened them. The cardboard journal bindings turned as brown as rolled cigars and the sentences blew away in cloudy rings of smoke. As my books burned, a fresh book opened within me—one to be scripted and polished by Gary.

I kept squirting on more and more lighter fluid until what written life I had placed onto those pages had burned down to silent ashes. Pictures blistered, and cards, stamps, newspaper clippings, tickets, bookmarks—all of it crumbled to smoldering cinders, and soon nothing remained of the arson but metal binders, paper clips, and blackened staples. It was very satisfying.

Yesterday when I climbed onto Gary's train I was riding along as swiftly and dangerously as he was. Then I realized I was just some scrap cargo on his back. But not anymore. Now I was only silence. And from silence I could shape myself into any word I wanted, and I wanted that word to be *Gary*.

INCOMING FIRE

For two days I didn't see Gary. I kept looking for him every chance I had. I went outside and washed and polished the Rambler. I cleaned the inside and scrubbed the wheels and all the time I listened for his voice, or his shoes scraping across the asphalt, but heard nothing. I constantly took out the trash and looked toward his house. I did the laundry for my mom so I could pin it up to dry on our backyard clothesline. To kill time I stood on our back porch and held an empty glass up to my mouth as if I were drinking. Secretly I was looking through the bottom of the glass as if it were a telescope. But I didn't spy him. Instead the round emptiness of the glass was like my own blank face spying on me. I closed my eyes. Where was he? Without him I was drifting back to my old pathetic Popeye self.

To buck myself up I imagined setting fires. I took out a box of matches I'd been carrying around in my back pocket. I opened the small drawer and plucked one out. I struck it on the box side. It flared up. The smell of sulfur burned the inside of my nose. I loved that smell and imagined holding the match to a handful of hay and setting Rome on fire. Burned it to the ground. I lit another and London went up in smoke. Then Tokyo. Chicago. Boston. San Francisco. Each match was another disaster. Washington. Atlanta. New York City. When I ran out of matches I was thirsty.

I was in the kitchen when he knocked on our front door. I could tell by the metal sound that it had to be the rings on his hand.

"I'll get it!" I hollered. When I opened the door he surprised me. He was dressed in a pair of khaki slacks and a white T-shirt and new Converse sneakers. He appeared more like me just as I tried to appear more like him.

But no matter how he dressed he was still Gary. "Hey, Sailor Jack," he said, and tugged a slender mother-of-pearl penknife from his pocket. "Can I use your phone?"

"Is yours broken?" I asked.

"I hate it when people ask me questions," he snapped back, and flicked open the blade. "But I'll tell you because it's funny. I racked up about a thousand dollars in phone calls talking to Leigh in Alabama and my dad can't pay the bill, so our phone is dead."

"You mean your girlfriend who drives the pickup?" I asked.

"Nicest girl in the world," he said, and ran his free hand back through his hair. "Never say anything bad about her," he advised, pointing the blade at me. "She's my savior and soon we're going to get married."

"My sister bakes really great cakes," I said. "You could hire her for the wedding. She could bake a cake that looks like your bride's truck on a highway."

"Or," he suggested as he peeled the curves of dirt from under his fingernails, "she could bake a cake of me making a phone call from your kitchen."

"Sorry," I said.

"I'll call her collect," he replied, nudging me. "I swear. Your parents won't know."

"My dad is probably up and he's a freak about phone charges."

"It's a collect call!" Gary said, and snapped the knife blade back into the handle. "It won't cost him a penny."

He dropped his head into his hands. "I feel a bad mood coming over me," he said in a distant voice, and lifted his right shoe, cocking it back like a nervous horse about to kick.

"Sorry," I said again. "When my parents leave you can do it."

"Forget it," he said, annoyed, and turned his face away as he quietly cursed over his shoulder.

When he suddenly turned back his mood seemed to have changed.

"Well, I got a more important favor to ask you anyway," he said, sounding upbeat.

"If I can do it I will," I said, relieved by the sudden shift in his mood.

"My probation officer is coming for an important house visit today—which is the reason I'm kind of dressed like you—and I was wondering if you could come over and be my friend, like, a new nice friend. Not like my old juvie friends, who can be a little too criminal."

"Yeah," I said enthusiastically. "I can be your new friend."

"Good," he replied, "and you won't be sorry. I only have a couple weeks left on probation, and my officer said I need to start hanging out with the type of people that make me a better person—like you."

"Me?" I said, and pointed to myself.

I didn't say it out loud, but my plan was that hanging around him would make me sort of a shadier person. Something more like his old friends.

"You do know right from wrong?" he asked. "It's an essential skill for the job."

"Sure," I said. "Of course I know right from wrong."

"Then you got the job!" he said cheerfully, and clapped his hands together. "You won't regret it. In fact, you can almost consider it a lifetime position."

"Perfect," I said. "Just what I was looking for."

At exactly the correct time I walked over to the Pagoda house. I was wearing an "after-church outfit," as my mom would have called it: brown slacks, a yellow tucked-in shirt, and penny loafers with dark socks.

I had my chess set with me and adjusted the box under one arm so I could ring their cracked plastic doorbell.

As soon as Gary jerked the front door open and I timidly stepped over the threshold, he slipped behind me and grabbed the back of my neck and bulled me headfirst down the hall and into a bathroom, where he shoved me up against a narrow wall between the box shower and stained toilet. He kicked the door closed behind us.

I crossed my arms over the chess set and held it flat against my belly as if it might shield me from a gut punch.

He seemed angry for no reason I could tell.

"What's wrong?" I asked, afraid even to say that much. I didn't dare say anything about him being in a bad *mood*. I'd already seen how that word always set him on fire.

He reached out and clamped his hand onto my chin and lined our eyes up. "I've just let you into my house, which means we are breaking new ground here," he said intensely. "I normally don't let people in, so this makes me nervous. But we don't have much time before the probation officer comes—now let's get our stories straight about our new neighborly friendship."

"Okay," I said. "I'll say anything you want."

"I like you, Sailor Jack, and I don't mind looking out for you, but don't cross me, because one word out of place and that dick can send me back to juvie. I'm close to the finish line with my probation, and I don't want to go all the way back to square one and have to shit in a bucket and eat cold grits and turnip greens three times a day."

"I'd never cross you," I said to him. "I've got your back."

And then I said what I had really been eager to say. "Count on me. I'm your right-hand man."

He smiled. "You are a lot of amusing things to me, but you are *not* my right-hand man," he said directly. "You are my shield against going back to juvie. In other words, you are not going to watch my back because you are my *face*. So, Mr. Face," he asked, "you ever been punched in the face?"

"No," I said, and quickly turned my cheek to one side. I knew what was coming.

"Look me in the eyes," he ordered, and lowered his hand to grip around my neck. "It won't hurt as much as you think."

The moment I straightened my chin out his fist hit me squarely on the mouth and my head snapped back against the wall. Stuff fell over in the shower and slid around out of sight.

"What do you taste?" he asked.

I licked my lip. "Blood," I replied.

"Good," he said. "But don't think of it as blood. It's vitamins. Blood is what makes you a man. And I need a man like you to be a good influence on me. You make me a better person in the eyes of my probation officer. You are the innocent Sea Cadet mask I get to wear. In other words, in the eyes of my probation officer you are going to make sure I know all my *rights* from all my *wrongs*."

"What's in it for me?" I asked.

"A question like that is very disappointing," he said in a slow, menacing way. "It makes me think you don't understand our relationship. So let's make this clear once and for all. *You*"—and he drove his finger into my chest—"get to be next to me. That's the gift I'm giving you in return. You got that?"

"Sure," I said, breathing harder. "Does that mean I get to end up being like you?"

"Don't be ridiculous," he said as he lit a cigarette. "Even if you could be me you don't want to be me. Heck, I don't even want to be me."

"Yes you do," I said quietly because I was a bit timid with what I was about to say. "I've given it a lot of thought. I want to be your double—kind of like a twin. Then you'd have someone just like yourself to hang out with."

He seemed amused by this. "You're a little stranger than I thought, Sailor Jack," he remarked. "But like I said, *maybe*. Someday you'll meet my friends and you'll see just how far you have to go to come up to our level."

I didn't like the thought of his friends. They'd just steal Gary's attention away from me. Maybe I could convince him not to see them. After all, my job was to give him good advice to keep him out of trouble.

Just then the doorbell rang.

"You going to be around later?" Gary asked.

"Yeah," I replied.

"Great," he said. "I have a little something for you—later."

"Like what?" I asked.

"*What!*" he shot back harshly. "I hate that word! Like when Alexander Graham Bell said, 'Mr. Watson, come here. I want to see you,' Watson didn't sit on his ass and whine, 'What ya need me for, boss?' Did he?"

"No," I said.

Gary blew cigarette smoke in my face. "Be like Watson and come when you are called. I already have parents who ruin my mood by asking *what* I'm doing. And now I have a probation officer crawling up my butt asking me *what*, so just either wait for me to show you *what* or go spend your time trying to be a girl with your sister and her friends." He reached out and grabbed the window curtain and handed it to me. "Wipe your mouth. You had a bathroom accident and you're bleeding."

"Gary!" Mrs. Pagoda sweetly called down the hallway as the house shifted a bit toward her. "Your

Mr. Mercier is here and I hope you filled out those papers."

"I did!" he hollered back, tossing his butt in the toilet and flushing.

Then he turned to me and leaned his forehead directly onto mine. His nose was against my nose. As he spoke his lips buzzed over my lips. "If in any way you screw this up for me I'll kill you. You know that grave I dug yesterday? Well, the last asshole who screwed me over is in there. So no funny business. Pay attention to me and agree with everything I say."

He pulled his face away, tousled my hair a bit, and gave me a shove forward. "Go be the fake good kid I know you are," he whispered. "Lie to my probation officer even better than you lie to your parents, yourself, or any girlfriend you might have had."

"Got it," I said, feeling anxious but eager to perform well in front of the probation officer. I was a pretty careful liar and once I got started I could slip one lie into another and into another like a nest of little boxes that all fit together.

When we entered the living room, Mrs. Pagoda was disappearing up the hallway. She moved like a slow billiard ball rolling toward a pocket and then she opened the door to a darkened den and rolled in. In the flickering light from a television, I could see Mr. Pagoda's feet resting on an ottoman, but I couldn't see the rest of him. Mrs. Pagoda closed the door behind her.

In the living room, Gary put his heavy hand on my shoulder to steady me. "Mr. Mercier," he said in a respectful voice, "meet my new friend, Jack Gantos."

Mr. Mercier was dressed in a baby-blue suit and white open-collared shirt and when we shook hands he held mine tightly enough to keep me from pulling away.

"Nice to meet you," he said crisply. "Do you have a record?"

I glanced at Gary. I was stupidly thinking of a record album.

"He's so clean," Gary said to Mr. Mercier, "that he doesn't even know what a 'record' means."

"You ever been to jail?" Mr. Mercier asked, giving my hand an extra squeeze. "You ever been busted for shoplifting? You ever skip school? You ever steal a bicycle?"

"No, sir," I said. "None of those things."

"Then why would you suddenly start hanging around with this criminal, who thinks *right* and *wrong* are the same word in the dictionary?"

He let go of my hand and began to crack his knuckles. If he had snapped my arm it wouldn't have sounded as loud as him cracking his thumb.

"Well," I said nervously, "because I'm really good at chess and he knows how to play and so we became chess friends." I was trying to sound convincing. "It's easy because we're next-door neighbors and he's nice—I mean, he doesn't cheat or anything."

"Gary," Mr. Mercier said, pivoting so quickly toward Gary I thought he was going to hit him with a sucker punch. "What's your favorite chess piece—the pawn or the queen?"

Gary pushed his hair away from his eyes. "The knight," he replied casually. "He's just like me. Two steps in one direction"—he took two steps forward—"and then one quick step off the deep end."

As he said that he turned to the side and dropped down onto one knee.

I laughed and the moment I did so Mr. Mercier regrabbed my hand, and very hard this time. He wanted to keep my mouth on a tight leash.

"So, Jack," he said, "how long have you known your new chess friend?"

I cut my eyes toward Gary. I knew he was aching to answer, and he jumped right in.

"Jack and I have been friends since he moved in next door."

Mr. Mercier let out a sigh of frustration.

"Jack," he said with more force, "how long have you lived next door?"

It had only been a few weeks.

"A month," Gary blurted out.

"Let the kid answer the questions," Mr. Mercier insisted, and slapped Gary across his leg.

"I've known Gary long enough," I said, "for him to join the Sea Cadets. My dad's the commodore."

"Is that like the Boy Scouts of the sea?" Mr. Mercier asked in a wise-guy voice.

"Yes," I said proudly. And then I turned to Gary. "By the way, your uniform just came in. Dad said he'll fit you up at the boathouse. He's got to sew your *accomplishment* patches on, and your name."

Mr. Mercier jerked my arm to get my full attention and looked at me with such contempt in his shiny eyes that I could stare back into them and see a faint image of myself being crushed by his scorn.

Suddenly he changed the conversation. "You have blood running out the side of your mouth."

He let go of my hand and pointed at my face as if I didn't know where my mouth was located.

I reached up and touched my lip where Gary had punched me. "I just had my braces removed," I explained, and wiped the blood on the back of my hand. "My gums are still sensitive."

"I have you pegged as a total fake," Mr. Mercier concluded in a voice practiced at being cold. "A serial liar like Gary doesn't hang around with little farts like you—little mama's boys."

Suddenly Gary was up on his toes. He stood like a boxer shifting his weight from side to side with his hands low and close to his hips, but his face was stretched all the way forward in anger.

"He's not a fake, Mr. M," he declared, spitting his words. "He's my friend, and he's helping me become a better person."

"Better for what?" Mr. Mercier asked. "Lying?"

Gary stepped toward him, and right then I stood and put my hand on Gary's shoulder, hoping to settle him down.

Mr. Mercier shrugged off Gary's performance. "Let me give you some advice," he said toward me, "just in case you are blind or retarded in some tragic way. Gary is a criminal sociopath who makes things disappear—starting with the truth. He's been in and out of foster care, juvie joints, and psych wards all his life. His brother, Frankie, has an IQ that doesn't add up to the coffee change in my pocket. The parents' nick-names are 'Don't Work' and 'Won't Work,' and only the sister, who is a dog groomer, keeps this family going on dented cans of baked beans and Alpo—and one of these days she'll wake up and ride off on a bullmastiff."

"I don't think so," I said. "They seem to me to be a whole family that sticks together."

"Yeah, like a box of rats are a whole family," he said sarcastically, and frowned. "Look, you seem like a nice kid," he said evenly. "Take my advice and walk out of this house and keep going." Once again he reached out and gripped my hand. "Any kid that enters this house will never leave as nice as when he arrived. You might think Gary'll end up being more like you, a mama's-boy-chess-king, but you will be more like him—a career criminal in his early years."

Then he didn't so much release my hand as throw it back at me—but this time it arrived with his business card folded into my fist. "You're playing with fire, kid. Do yourself a favor and leave. Now."

I looked at Gary.

Gary pointed toward the front door. "You heard the man. Go," he said insistently. "Save yourself from me.

You ever knock on my door again I'll knock you unconscious." He lunged at me with a mock punch.

I ducked anyway. "What about the Sea Cadets?" I asked. "My dad paid in advance for that uniform."

"Tell him to call the admiral for a refund. Now beat it."

I walked quickly out of his house, leaving the chess set behind, and crossed the crackling grass shards toward my front door.

I was embarrassed and angry. All I could do was think of vengeful little things like holding Gary's head down in the canal and letting one of those Korean fish chew his face off. That would be satisfying. Or I could call the cops and have them dig up Gary's side yard looking for bodies.

I grabbed my front doorknob and held it for a moment. Then I froze.

Was Gary pulling a fast one on me? I couldn't tell. He had changed so quickly from almost punching Mr. Mercier to then threatening me.

I went into our house and from behind our curtain I watched out my living room window and as soon as Mr. Mercier drove off in his Ford Falcon I went running back over to Gary's house.

This time I knocked on the door. He pulled it open and gave me a quick punch to the face like a fist popping out of a cuckoo clock. I shot straight back onto my ass.

"Did I not tell you to keep your mouth shut?" he said.

"But I didn't do anything wrong," I whined, and rubbed my lips.

"Which is why I only gave you a love tap on your kisser . . . for being so *sensational.* I gotta pay you back for that performance. I owe you one. He didn't believe a word you said. Every word gave him indigestion. But he couldn't catch you in a lie. Now let's go have some fun," he said, taking two steps forward and one to the side. "I thought of a new game for the Pagoda Olympics of the Future."

FIRE AWAY

He hollered for his brother and sister and they appeared from somewhere and followed us out of the house.

He strolled across his yard and across the street, where he began to tug on the brass corner grommets of a giant canvas tarp that covered some kind of vehicle.

In a minute we could see a shiny new Broward County Police tow truck. There wasn't a spot on it.

"Where'd you get that?" I whispered. "Out of the factory paint shop?"

"What did I tell you about asking questions?" he replied. "Remember the juvie code: To stay safe is to stay stupid."

He opened the passenger front door and pulled out a chain saw and a can of gasoline.

"Just watch," he said, "and learn from the master of the new Olympic Games."

In their front yard they had a tall, whippy-looking Australian pine tree—the kind that wasn't like a Christmas tree, but more like a thin southern pine with pinkish bark and a flexible trunk. The branches stuck out from either side of the trunk like long furry dog tails that wagged this way and that in the breeze. The needles hung down limply like rows of knotted green ribbon.

It was an odd tree and very delicate and beautiful—more of an exotic musical instrument from another century, a strange kind of magical harp. Its beauty seemed out of place at the Pagoda house and now it appeared to be a very nervous tree, shaking all the time like one of those shivering Italian greyhounds that, even in Florida, were dressed in sweaters. As it turned out, it should have been nervous.

"It's the destiny of trees to give their lives for our pain and pleasure," Gary announced, and made the sign of the cross in its direction.

He gassed up the chain saw and pulled the starter cord. Instantly the nasal, angry growl of the saw lashed out in circles at the air. Gary held it over his head as if gutting the sky and walked up to the tree and quickly began to cut through the lower branches. He left about six inches of each branch attached to the trunk. As he pruned a branch above himself he could next step up to that stub. He used the stubs like rungs on a ladder, with the screaming saw spitting out wood chips over his head and into his hair.

The smell of the pine was refreshing. I had become used to the constant rotting stench of the canal.

Gary ascended that tree one step after the other, as easily as a telephone man climbs a pole. It was impressive. When he reached the top of the tree, which was about twice as tall as the peaked roof of their single-story house, he sliced off the elaborate headdress of unfurling new branches and leaves. Then he choked the saw off and began to descend one notch at a time.

The saw swung in his hand like it was a weapon and he was the big-game hunter who had just felled a giraffe.

"Frankie," he ordered on the way down, "collect all those branches and stack them up so we can use them to camouflage the tow truck."

"Alice," he called out, "get me that big spool of nylon rope we use for tripping up water-skiers."

She ran back into the garage and in a moment came out with a plywood spool with about fifty yards of heavy yellow boat rope. She rolled it down the driveway, and Frankie and I helped her push it across the grass.

Once Gary was on the ground he hung the saw by its handle on the lowest peg. He peered up at the naked tree, which looked like a stubby toothpick.

We peered up at it, too.

"So, Olympic athletes, here is what we are going to do," he announced. "I will tie the rope onto the top of the tree, supertight, and then one of you will climb to the top and hang on to the tree like a koala bear. I will take the loose end of the rope and tighten it around the winch on the tow truck, and when the tree is bent backward—having been aimed toward a certain valuable target—I will let the rope go and the tree will snap forward. You must time your release from the treetop in order to hit your target destination.

"Here are some tips. If you release too soon, you will shoot straight up into the air and come straight down. If you hang on too long and the tree snaps way forward, it will fling you facedown on the ground. So consider the geometry and timing that may shape, or misshape, your future."

I tried to keep my expression blank so as not to show any fear.

"Finally, I must tell you. There are only three targets and you have to pick one. There is an easy one, a harder one, and an insanely deadly one. You got that?"

I sort of did. "What are the targets?" I asked.

"Asking a question," Gary said, "is against game rules—thus you will have to go first. So, big mouth, here are your choices: A, I will catapult you over the roof of our crappy little house and you will hope to land alive in the swimming pool. B, the kiddie pool near the tree in the side yard is full of water and those Korean death fish, and you will have to land dead-center in that to avoid breaking your face. And C, looking toward the other side of the yard is a very friendly southern oak tree with lots of soft Spanish moss covering the branches. This is the easy one. I shoot you in there, and all you have to do is grab a branch and hang on."

I raised my hand. "Can I ask another question?"

He groaned. "If I lived with you I'd smother you in your sleep."

"Since each target is so different," I continued, "are the rewards or prizes better for the harder ones?"

"Indeed," he said, and smiled appreciatively. "I've built that into the game. Each target has a prize that is calibrated to please one exact person. So if you are shot blindly over the house and land in the pool, then at a very future date you can join me and my friends at a special private juvie-reunion party where all sorts of fun may just be lurking about. Or, if you land in the Korean killer-fish pool, you can have my brass knuckles. Or, if you land in the oak tree, you can have my plush, three-foot-high pink teddy bear and I promise I will remove my ex's name from the bear's rear end because I will never have anything to do with Tomi and her lying ways in the future."

He took the end of the rope and quickly climbed the tree and tied it to the top, then returned with the other end of the rope and yanked it to the tow truck and got it hooked to the winch cable.

Since I had first choice, I couldn't resist trying to win an invite to the juvie-reunion party. Even though I was a little jealous of his outlawed friends I was thrilled he would give me a chance to meet them.

"I go for the swimming pool," I announced.

Frankie snorted through his nose. "I better call an ambulance now," he said gleefully. "Or a hearse."

I trotted toward the tree as Gary backed the tow truck into position so that it was in a straight line with the roof and pool. It was easy to climb the tree, and as I made my way up I could feel that the trunk was very strong and yet very springy. It was also pretty tall, and I figured my best approach would be to let go a little early and lob myself in a soft arc over the house and into the pool's deep end. When I reached the top of the tree I could see just enough of the back patio to imagine the pool's location, and that helped me figure out my flight path.

Once I got myself turned around into a position where I thought I would be able to let go at the right time, I gave Gary a hand signal. He started the tow truck and began to winch the rope in. I could hear the cracking stress compression in the wood as the top of the tree was pulled back.

Before long the tree was bent over and I was staring upward at the blue sky and my heart was pounding. It suddenly occurred to me my chances of making the pool were slim, but I did not regret any of what was about to happen even if I hit the diving board or the tiled edge of the pool. If taking a chance like this would bring me closer to Gary and his juvie pals, then I had to do it. I had to be more to him than just the face of his choirboy friend every time Mr. Mercier visited. That was not good enough.

When Gary had me bent back to about fifteen feet off the ground he yelled out, "Ready to meet your maker?"

Frankie was saying "Holy shit!" and slapping himself all over like he was invisibly on fire. He looked psychotic, but then again I was preparing to be catapulted from a tree, over a house, and into a pool I couldn't see. I silently waved my arm and a moment later Gary severed the yellow line with bolt cutters.

The tree had a lot of instant power and it felt as if I were sitting on a giant flyswatter that some monster had pulled back and let loose. I quickly elevated and cleared the house, which I never thought would be a problem. It was landing in the deep end of the pool that was going to take a miracle.

For a moment it appeared I had too much speed and was going to shoot well beyond the pool and maybe cannonball badly onto the stinking bank of trash thrown by the canal, or into the nasty canal sludge water, where I'd just get stuck and be slowly eaten by the Korean death fish.

I only spent milliseconds torturing myself with each particular fear, and yet each tragic story of my crash, death, and funeral seemed to take hours to unfold in my mind.

But my geometry was well planned, and as I approached the pool my acceleration slowed and I ran out of forward momentum and dropped.

I plunged straight down into the water and hit the concrete pool bottom hard but not so hard that I crushed my ankles, and then I pushed up. When I broke the surface I was smiling crazily because I had done it. I had been terrified but I'd lived! It *was* miraculous. And what's more, even though I doubted myself, Gary must have known I could do it. He was just grooming me to be on his regular level—and be better than his juvie friends.

Alice was the spotter on the pool side and when I broke water on the surface she waved her rubbery limbs over her head and shouted out through her undersized sea urchin mouth to Frankie and Gary, as they came running around the side of the house, "I can't believe he did it! You didn't kill him, which is really what I wanted to happen."

Then she turned to me. Her little teeth were like pencil points.

"You got lucky, kid, but you can't live on luck forever."

I didn't know her at all. This was the first thing she had ever said to me, but after she revealed her blood wish I knew she was a purebred Pagoda—a special morbid breed of dog that trackers use to hunt down the tragic events caused by disturbed people.

I trotted over to Gary and he was grinning from ear to ear.

"Dang," he said. "I thought for sure I would have executed you and that would be the end of all your nonstop questions."

"Nope," I said, grinning grandly. "I'm alive and all I need now are some juvie party clothes."

"That would be called shoplifting," Gary informed me. "Probably the first low-rung skill a juvie kid develops."

"Is that an assignment?" I asked, knowing that I was going to start shoplifting one way or the other.

"One more question and I blast you into the electric wires," he replied, and pointed toward the high power lines that ran overhead. I imagined that birds landing on them would burst into flames.

Frankie was next up for the contest. He chose the fish pool. Gary repositioned the truck, reattached the line, and winched him back. Frankie let go a little too late and he flew low across the yard like a lawn dart. He hit the ground early and ricocheted off the pool as he plowed up the ground with his chest and some of the skin on his lower chin. He finished his assault on the killer fish with a somersault and hopped up onto both feet.

"*Voilà!*" he hollered in a voice that did not sound victorious. Then his hand reached for his chin because it looked like he had a broken jaw.

But the jaw was just stunned and he wiggled it back into working order while snapping his teeth together like toy windup dentures.

"I'm not doing any more of these Pagoda Olympic Games," he said, pouting. "It's insane, but do I get the brass knuckles anyway?"

"Of course not," Gary replied. "In the Olympics you get either a gold, silver, or bronze medal. There is no *brass* medal. You screwed up. If you want to try again I'll give you a second chance. Two *brass* attempts will win a bronze."

"Let me get some Band-Aids first," Frankie whimpered, and headed toward the house. "And a helmet."

"No helmets allowed," Gary fired back. "You know the rules."

"Then I quit," said Frankie as he disappeared inside.

"My turn," Alice said, perking up. "Just give me a soft shot into the oak tree. It looks easy—plus I want the pink teddy bear."

It *was* easy. She climbed the tree and he gently lobbed her in. She crashed through a few outer branches, which were as spongy as old rope, and she ended up grabbing hold of a vertical branch that she could hug.

While she stayed in the tree, Gary went inside and got the teddy bear for her. He came out and tossed it up to her along with his cigarette lighter.

"Burn the name off the butt end," he said. "It's yours now."

"You'd better think quick," she said. "From up here I see a cop car a few blocks away."

"Crap," Gary replied. "Quick, Sailor Jack, grab the tarp and meet me behind the garage."

He jumped in the truck and it roared to life. He raced it down the strip of dead grass and ivy between his house and the neighbors' driveway since they weren't home. I met him around back and helped him throw the tarp over the truck.

Then we dashed back for the branches and chucked those on top.

When that was done I ran for my backyard and hid behind a tree where I could watch the scene.

A few minutes later, the cop pulled up to Gary, who was casually spooling the rope in his front yard. It was the same cop as before.

"Hey, did you find Flame-Out?" Gary asked.

The cop didn't seem amused. "The department is missing a tow truck," he said roughly. "Someone said they saw it around here. You got it? Because I know you have a special thing for tow trucks."

"Never seen it," Gary said. He was a good liar. He kept his answers simple and he always denied everything.

The cop stared blankly at him, and then turned toward his squad car. "I try to be nice to you, but you won't be straight with me," he said with contempt. "Every tip you give me is a dead end."

"What do you expect from a guy who has been labeled a dead end all his life?" Gary shot back, telling the truth with the same voice he told lies. Maybe they were the same to him.

Suddenly from the tree where Alice was sitting came the *whoosh* of a flame and Alice squawked like one of those electrocuted birds and the flaming teddy bear dropped to the ground and in seconds it had melted down to a bubbling puddle of brownish-pink gunk and black smoke.

The cop had a startled look on his face and then he frowned and abruptly shoved his gearshift in reverse, did a screeching three-point turn, and peeled rubber down to the corner.

I ran over to Gary.

"I gotta get this thing out of here," Gary said, and walked quickly toward the tow truck.

I followed close behind.

"Are you going to be okay?" I asked.

I was hoping he'd want me to come with him.

"Actually, I'm more worried about you," he said, and held me at bay by the front of my wet shirt. "The girl who lives on the other side of you returned last week."

He pointed to the house next to ours—the one with the empty swimming pool.

"I haven't seen a girl there," I said.

"Don't question me," he snapped. "Just listen to your master's voice. There is a girl in there. She's hiding just now because she told everyone a lot of lies about me, and now she's afraid of me. But as soon as I'm gone she'll surface. She'll see you and size you right up. She's beautiful. You won't be able to stay away from her. But you have to."

"Why?"

He slapped my face fast and hard.

"That's another word I don't like. Just accept that she's smarter than you," he said as a fact. "And that you'll fall in love with her and believe everything she says."

"Not the lies," I said.

"Especially the lies," he replied. "Now, I'm in a hurry, if you haven't noticed."

He squatted down and began to unbolt the back license plate on the tow truck.

I leaned over him.

"What's her name?" I asked.

"You don't need to know. You'll say it just once and like a genie she'll appear and ruin your life."

He began to bolt on a fake license plate from Georgia.

"I'm good with girls," I said with confidence. "I can resist her. I've resisted girls all my life."

"Not by choice," he said deliberately. "They've actually resisted you all your life."

He handed me a can of white spray paint.

"Now, shut up and listen. Spray over all the lettering on the passenger-side door. And not another word out of you."

I did my side while he did his. When he finished, I finished. I tossed the spray paint in the passenger side as he hopped up on the driver's seat and slammed his door.

I jumped up on the running board and watched as he bent forward around the wheel, crossed two wires under the dashboard, and started the engine.

"Just remember this," he said. "Once a girl loves me she's never allowed to love anyone else—ever. They just become my harem-of-the-unhappy."

I didn't know how to reply to that as I jumped off the running board and he reversed down the side yard onto the driveway. I chased after him as he hit the street, curling the back end of the truck around, and by the time he straightened the wheel and hit the gas he was already in second gear and at the far corner. He didn't slow down as he took the turn, and once he shifted into third he was out of sight.

I walked over to my yard wondering if I'd ever see him again because he said he was going to marry his Alabama girlfriend and if he did and stayed up there I'd be stuck with just myself. Or maybe that genie would show up and I could pretend I was the new Gary. Maybe she'd like me then and call me "Master."

HEAT-TREATED

After Gary left I felt like a hermit crab that had lost its protective shell. But as it turned out I didn't have to wait long to find a girl who liked improving boys.

Gary was only gone a couple hours when the girl next door spotted me, just as he said she would. But since I was becoming more like him, it seemed right that she would want to meet me.

I was holding a metal bucket full of ashes from the papers and journals I had burned in the grill. I was thinking of my own burned remains when a high-pitched voice called out, "Hey, you."

I turned and looked across our dead yard toward the chain-link fence between us and the other side neighbor.

A girl stood there.

I turned away and threw the ashes into the nasty canal. They spread across the surface like a burn scar. Then I turned back in her direction.

"Hey," she said, a little more confidently now that she'd caught my eye. "Over here!"

She waved her hand back and forth like a child waving a little parade flag. She had to be the girl Gary did not want me to talk to, but she seemed so nice and innocent.

I liked her immediately, even if I didn't have the words to describe why. I probably should have looked uninterested at that moment and walked away, but Gary had said that once I saw her I wouldn't be able to stay away from her, so I was just following his prediction.

"Hey," she said again, and stood up on her toes. "I'm talking to you, so don't ignore me."

I just stood there feeling my heart beat. She was his ex-girlfriend and must have given him the pink teddy bear with her name, Tomi, written on it. She looked like a genie with a triple bun of brown hair and a round face and eyes as if she were from the Far East—Singapore or Jakarta—someplace exotic where it was possible to be a saffron sunrise of light captured in a bottle and end up released as a sunset in Florida. That seemed impossible, but I guess the impossible was just what I wanted. I waved back to her as I thought to myself, *Her hair is stacked up like a pagoda.*

"Come over here and help me, please?" she asked politely. "I just want to ask you something."

The way she leaned over the fence reminded me of a petting zoo where the animals know you have food in your hand and so they stretch their long necks and chests forward and push a bulge in the fence until it looks like it might just split apart.

It wasn't only the way she pressed against the fence either. She had the kind of magnetic force my dad or uncles or older guys would talk about when they talked about trouble with women.

"Come on," she said, and waved her hand at me. "I want to talk to you. Don't be such a shy guy." And her eyes and chin and smile sort of bobbed up and down with that joy of being alive, like a newborn pony.

I don't know why I kept thinking of her as if she were a beautiful animal because she was so obviously a beautiful girl, but anything in nature that is beautiful is pure, and she seemed pure. Maybe that's what I was thinking without putting the right words to it.

I glanced over at the Pagoda house even though I knew Gary was long gone. Then I took one step toward her, and the other steps followed.

I squinted and tilted my face forward because the sun was reflecting off the aluminum flashing along the edge of her roof and the ray of light was hitting me in the eyes. With my face bent to the ground she may have thought I was approaching her as if she were a goddess and I was unworthy of looking her in the eyes. She wouldn't have been all that wrong.

As I walked across the crunchy brown lawn, darting waves of grasshoppers fled from around my shoes. It was as if I were splashing water—or walking on water. Maybe she was some kind of genie and had already put a grasshopper spell on me.

When I got closer to her fence the sun was blocked out by the roof overhang and I stepped into a shadow. I raised my eyes. "Yes?" I said.

"Did you see those grasshoppers?" she asked with some amazement.

I smiled. "Yes," I said, nodding.

"They were beautiful," she remarked. "When the light hit them they looked like colored glass."

"I was squinting," I said, "and couldn't see that." I glanced over at Gary's house again. His warning was pretty magnetic, too.

"Do you have a cigarette?" she asked, and held two fingers across her lips as if she were taking a puff of one. She had very nice lips and *they* looked like colored glass.

"I don't smoke," I said, and shrugged.

"That's not what I asked," she replied. "Can you get a cigarette? I'll split it with you."

"We don't have any," I replied, and for some crazy reason I said, "And my friend Gary isn't around or I'd get some from him."

Suddenly the cigarettes were uninteresting to her. "I know you know Gary," she said in a singsong way, and shifted her weight from one leg to the other. "Well, I know him, too," she said, but with a little venom.

"He lives next door," I said stupidly, and nodded toward his house.

"Don't I know it," she shot back. "I've been there one too many times, if you know what I mean."

She said that like she knew him in a special way. I could feel myself getting jealous because I wanted her to know me in a special way.

"Well, can you go get me some cigarettes?" she asked nicely. "I have the money and I figure you have a bike."

"Sure," I agreed. I had nothing else to do. I didn't have to mow the grass, although Dad did say I should rake it so that it looked like combed hair on a flat head. He was joking at first and then he talked himself into saying, "Sculpt it into a navy insignia—like an anchor." He showed me the crest on his navy ring for a template.

Suddenly the girl turned on one foot, like a dancer.

"I'll be right back," she said. "Let me get the money."

I stood there watching her quickly run toward her back door and she looked more like a woman than a girl. Maybe that's when I should have run toward my back door so that Gary wouldn't know a thing. But I stayed like a little puppy eager to please her as my eyes mindlessly drifted toward the Pagoda house.

She returned faster than I expected. When she got to the fence she looked at me like she was about to laugh.

"What?" I asked.

"Nothing," she remarked. "It's just that you're staring at that house like it's after you."

"No," I said, hiding my thoughts behind a lie.

She held out a man's wallet. "There are a few leftover bucks in there," she said. "Get something for yourself."

"That's okay," I said. "I'm fine."

"Well, when you come back I'll tell you a story about that wallet," she said pointedly, and dipped her head as a silent promise. "And that will be your reward."

"I'd like that," I managed to say, which led me to ask, "What's your name?"

I asked even though I knew.

"Tomi King," she said. "I'm quarantined to my house because I just flew home on a plane and some baby had whooping cough or the measles or the plague, so I'm not allowed to spread it—if I have it, that is."

I covered my mouth as if I were yawning, but it was because of the germs. I was a little like my mother when it came to the fear of germs. I turned my head to one side and took a deep breath.

"Pick any brand," she said. "I like surprises."

"I'll be back soon," I said, and trotted around to the front of my house and hopped on my bicycle.

I pedaled down to Gus's Gas Station in a jiffy. He charged kids more for cigarettes than adults, but that was okay. It wasn't my money. When I opened the wallet to pay I saw there was a corner of paper folded over into the license slot. I pulled it out and examined it. It was a pilot's license. The name on it was Johnny Foil.

I didn't know what to think of that, but Tomi had said she'd tell me the story, so I hopped back on my bike and headed home.

She was waiting for me right where I had left her and she waved her hand in that flag-waving way like before and it felt so good to have someone happy to see me.

"Hi," she called out as I marched toward her in a straight line as if I had no choice.

I held up the pack of cigarettes.

"Oh, Kents!" she said, and clapped her hands together. "My favorite."

She reached across the fence for them, but I held them just beyond her grasp. "Are you going to tell me the story of this wallet?" I asked. "Like you promised?"

"You read my mind," she said, and I put the Kents and a pack of matches in her soft, open hand.

"Do you know Suzy Pryor?" she asked, and sat down on her side of the fence.

"She's my sister's best friend," I replied, and slowly sat down on my prickly grass.

"Good," she said as she opened the cigarette package and plucked one out with her long nails. She lit it, inhaled, exhaled, and pulled her shoulders way back as if she were a bow ready to launch an arrow. And then she did.

Very quickly she said, "I didn't like Suzy very much. But now I do and I'll tell you why in a minute. So Gary had a 'thing' for Suzy, but she didn't care for him and his ways. She had a boyfriend—a rich kid named Jordan Abernathy. She met him at church. Anyway, he would show up in a shiny black Lincoln driven by a chauffeur and the chauffeur would park in Suzy's driveway and open the door for Jordan, and then

Jordan would stroll up to her front door with flowers and call on Suzy. It was pretty weird for around this crappy neighborhood but really nice, too, because Jordan was a good guy even though he was like Richie Rich in the comics. He was cute, though not that cute, but his money made up the difference. Well, because Jordan was really nice to Suzy and gave her gifts and took her to good restaurants Gary got all worked up. He claimed Suzy was just after the money and all and was using Jordan, and if anyone else came around with some money she'd leave Jordan in a split second. Gary was just plain old jealous because he didn't have any money, and his smile and those awful shoes and that motorcycle jacket weren't getting him anywhere.

"And then the most amazing thing happened. Just over by Gus's Gas Station, across the street, is an old abandoned golf course."

"The fenced-in one," I quickly remarked, having just passed it on my bike ride.

"It's all grown over—like a jungle," she added. "I used to go there with a lot of friends and hang out. Well, an airplane movie was being filmed above it so that the planes would look like they were flying over Africa or the Amazon or somewhere lush. There were three airplanes. Two were old World War I biplanes and the other was a modern camera plane. Anyway, the old planes were flying this way and that, pretending to have a battle, when something went wrong and one of the biplanes brushed wings with the camera plane. And that biplane came crashing down on the golf course. The other two planes made it back to the airport, but the third plane blew up when it hit the ground.

"As it turns out, Gary was over there because that's where he used to hang out instead of going to school. So he sees it hit and runs toward it. The plane was made of canvas and wood, and with the fuel tank smashed open it was all on fire. Gary spotted the pilot in his seat and he was on fire too, and trapped in the wreck. So Gary runs into the fire, grabs the burning pilot, and pulls him out. But he was dead. So Gary being Gary he took the guy's wallet."

"Johnny Foil," I guessed.

"Yep," she replied, and then said, "I could use another cigarette." She seemed to take her time getting the second cigarette out of the pack, but when she did she lit it right up.

Once she exhaled she slowly shrugged as if the story were pressing down on her shoulders. "Anyway, there was a thousand dollars in the wallet because that's what the movie people paid the pilot. The police spread the word about the missing wallet because the theft was so foul. But Gary didn't take a cent of the money and he goes and gives it to Suzy and says to her, 'Now you don't need Richie Rich. You got your own money and a *real* man. So forget him because you are mine now.'

"She didn't go for that. She just told him, 'I'll stick with Jordan.' So Gary leaves the wallet on her doorstep and walks away angry. Well, nobody knows what happened next, but Jordan mysteriously stops coming around for Suzy. Someone said Gary threatened him and he went running off to boarding school or something. And Suzy told me this really good part—she took the full wallet and hid it and then told Gary that if he ever bothered her again she'd call the police and show them the wallet and tell them that he stole it and gave it to her. She thought it was pretty sick that he thought he could just buy her love with a dead man's money. Her hiding the wallet was pretty smart because that threat kept Gary from bothering her and so he started looking around for another girlfriend."

Then she paused and took a long drag on her Kent. "Well, without going into details, something happened between me and Gary and I got pregnant." She looked away from me after she said that.

"What?" I said quietly, maybe sounding a little confused. Or young. Or stupid.

"Don't make me explain the birds and the bees," she said, as if she were tired.

"Was it Gary?" I asked, knowing it would be, but I just had to hear her say so.

"Who else?" she sort of groaned. "And so I was in big trouble last year and my parents don't have any money and I needed to be sent away to this depressing place for unwed mothers to have the baby. Gary vanished into some juvie joint, so he was no help. We didn't know what to do. Hide me indoors for nine months? Then Suzy shows up at my front door one night, really late, and hands me the wallet. 'This should belong to you,' she said. 'And I'm really sorry because he's a creep.'

" 'He is,' I said to her. 'He sure is.'

" 'I didn't spend a cent of it,' Suzy says. 'It makes me sick just to have had it.'

"She was an angel to me. So I got the wallet and took out the cash and I told my parents 'the boy' gave it to me and they were so desperate they didn't want to know the truth—but they knew deep down it wasn't right. So I got sent off for months and had the baby and it went to a nice family and now here I am—right back where I started." She lit another cigarette.

"So that's a true story?" I asked.

"Of course it is," she said, raising her voice. "I wouldn't lie about all that just for a cigarette."

At that moment her mother leaned out the sliding door. "Tomi," she called. "It's time to come in for a while and help with supper."

"Okay," Tomi called back over her shoulder. Then quickly she turned to me with the wallet in her outstretched hand. "So I gave you that story. It's like a special gift, and now I want you to give me a gift in return—I want you to give this back to Gary," she said intently. "Put it in his hands and ask him what it means, and see if he has the you-know-whats to tell you the truth as I have. And if he lies, then I don't think you'll want to be his friend much longer."

Then she stood up and smiled at me and slowly patted my hand like I was a special pet. "Well, thanks for getting me the smokes," she said, then headed for her door but not before she paused and looked back at me over her shoulder. "See you around," she said, and I knew I wanted to be seen.

I stood up and headed for our door, realizing that she'd just told me that if I got rid of Gary I could be her friend. That was something to think about because she was so nice and honest and all the warmer feelings

I shared with my mother were stirring inside me like a soft pet circling before lying down for a nap. And there were other feelings too, but those I kept to myself.

When I entered the house my sister was just inside the door and glaring at me with her hands on her hips.

"You should leave that girl alone," she said firmly. "She's a nice girl."

"I'm a nice guy," I replied smoothly. "I was just talking to her."

"Well, I've been told she's had a rough time lately, so no funny business," she warned.

"What do you mean by that?" I asked.

"Keep your hands to yourself," she replied. "Growing up is hard enough without creeps pulling you down." Then she turned and retreated to her room, and when she closed her door it was like putting the period on the end of a sentence.

RING OF FIRE

My dad walked by while I was doing what I had been doing a lot of lately—staring out our dining room window. Mom and I had just gotten back from grocery shopping and I was restless. I had been looking at the Pagoda house to see if Gary had returned so I could ask him about the wallet, which was in my pocket. I kept touching it and soon I was looking at Tomi's house to see if she was smoking out by the fence and just waiting for me to ask Gary about the wallet.

Maybe she figured Gary would be so pissed off at me that he'd dump me as a friend and I'd be all hers. Maybe not. Maybe he'd only slap me around for talking to her in the first place and she'd never talk to me again.

Then I looked at Gary's house some more, and then hers. I may have been craning my neck back and forth for an hour or more wondering what was going to happen now that I was in the middle. I had to make a choice, but I just kept wringing my hands.

That's when my dad walked by and said, "Hey, Popeye, why don't you do something useful besides waiting like a loser for that Pagoda kid to show up in his jockey shorts?" Then he reached out and flicked me on the top of my head with his big navy ring. "That kid seems like trouble anyway."

"Ow!" I said, and rubbed the sore spot on my skull. "He's not that much trouble. He actually wants to join the Sea Cadets, and I was thinking we should invite him to the weekend retreat at Birch State Park."

"Really?" he asked, and bugged his eyes out. "That's a surprise. Does he know we aren't a bunch of Barbary pirates?"

"I told him all about the cadets," I replied. "He said he loves nature and boating and joining clubs, and it would be good to recruit a new member."

"Why not?" Dad reasoned. "He can't be any more useless than his old man, who I see down at the VFW clubhouse. He was with the marines in the South Pacific during the war—he told me that's where he got that goofy Pagoda last name. His family name is Komodo, like the giant lizard. During a battle he was on the USS *Dale* in the Komodo Straits to attack the Japanese when they hit a reef and ripped a hole in their ship. He got tagged with being bad luck because of his name and so somehow they started calling him Pagoda instead and after the war he made the change official."

"Is that true?" I asked. "That sounds made-up."

"Who knows?" Dad said. "There was a battle there, but the guy is a complete nut. After a few drinks that Shriners fez drops down over his eyes like it's a red fire bucket on his head."

"Maybe it's his battle helmet," I quipped.

"Yeah, for falling off his bar stool," Dad added.

After that exchange I went outside and raked the yard so the grass was all slanting in one direction. I had seen a photograph of a meteor that hit Siberia with such explosive force that all the trees for miles around were slanted in the same direction. I think that was one of the pictures I had burned. I wished I hadn't burned it, because now that I thought about it I liked that picture. I always imagined myself as a flea on a dog and the trees were the dog's fur going in one direction.

Really what I wished for most of all was that I could do something on my own instead of always looking for someone else to hang around with. Before my dad caught me staring out the window my sister had walked by and called me a "little lost puppy-boy." Maybe I needed a real puppy to take care of so everyone would stop calling me a puppy. But I knew that wouldn't happen because of the baby and because we had already given away three dogs because of all our moving.

I went over to the Pagodas' garage, where I thought Alice might be working at her dog salon. Maybe she'd let me help her wash and groom the dogs. And then maybe if I was really helpful she'd find someone who wanted to give one away and I could secretly get it and keep it at her house. That was wishful thinking, but if I had a pet to love me I could love it back and nothing could come between us. Maybe that was the best relationship in the world and I wouldn't be staring out the window all day like a puppy looking for an owner.

When I turned the corner behind the garage, Frankie and Alice were sitting on the rubber seats of an old metal swing set. A bored-looking Yorkie was sleeping in the dirt next to Alice. The seats were hanging by rusty chains that made a high-pitched grinding sound as they swung back and forth. It made my head hurt.

The two of them looked pretty gloomy, but when they saw me they perked right up, which perked me up.

"You're just the guy we are looking for," Alice said with her little round mouth grinding her sawblade teeth back and forth.

I couldn't stop looking at her mouth. The other day it had reminded me of a sea urchin. Now it looked like a meat grinder for making sausages.

"He'll do," Frankie said, and hopped off his seat, which made the chains screech so loudly I grimaced.

I tried to ignore him.

"I just came over to look at the dogs," I said to Alice. "I was wondering if I could play with them. I really want a puppy, but we can't have one right now." I kept the reason to myself.

"We just got some new pups," she said. "A lady dropped her spaniel off to be boarded for a few weeks, and first thing the dang girl went around the corner and had five little pups. And nothing is cuter than a baby spaniel."

"Can I see them?" I said.

"Only if you do something first," she insisted. "We're working on a deadly new Olympic game called Ring of Fire and we need another person to make it work.

Gary thought it up, but he's still in Alabama getting married. But now that you are here we can try it."

"Can I have a spaniel?" I asked. "I don't want to die for nothing."

"Okay," she said. "I'll give you one of them. The lady won't know if one is missing—I'll tell her there were only four."

"Can I keep it here?" I asked. "My parents don't want one at the house."

"Okay," she said impatiently. "You can keep it over here for a boarding price. We have a dozen dogs as it is."

"Yeah, just look at the yard," Frankie pointed out. "It's nothing but dog poop."

There was a lot of poop—and green-eyed flies buzzing around low to the ground.

"Is the game dangerous?" I asked stupidly, knowing it would have to be since Frankie hadn't called it a "totally safe and harmless Pagoda Olympic game."

"You may be maimed for life, but I figure you won't die," Alice said irritably. "But if you do I promise we won't bury you under the poop." She pointed to a fenced-in area with a lot of little wooden grave markers.

"That's my pet cemetery," Frankie piped in. "I carve all the little crosses and dog faces by hand."

"Gary said you were talented," I remarked.

He grinned. "It's a special skill," he said proudly. "I've always been good with a carving knife."

"Okay," I said to Alice, wanting to get on with it so I could pick out which puppy would be mine. But there was something about playing with these two little idiots that made me feel like an idiot. "What do I have to do to get this over with?"

In a few minutes I was sitting on the top of the tall sheet-metal slide attached to the swing set. It was rusty, too, and sort of leaning perilously to the left where the legs had sunk down to their knees into the sandy soil.

Frankie had that side propped up a bit with a few two-by-fours to keep it somewhat stable, but it was still tilted.

Once I was in position, I had to put on a pair of metal roller skates—the adjustable kind you stepped into and fastened over your sneakers with clamps that tightened down with a skate key.

Down below, the end of the slide was propped up on bricks. I took a few practice runs and after each one Frankie kept stacking more bricks under the lip of the slide. "You need more elevation," he said. "To look like a real daredevil."

When he was happy with the height of my jumps, Frankie ran to the garage and returned with some other equipment. He had an oversized pink-and-white swirly plastic hula hoop and he started wrapping it with a roll of cotton gauze the way you might wrap a wounded soldier's bleeding limb to keep him from dying.

Alice was playing with a Polaroid camera. She took a shot of the Yorkie she should have been grooming. After a minute she held up the photograph. "The film is no good," she called over to Frankie. "Look, it's blurry."

He looked at it. "Better get the movie camera," he said. "I think this is going to be a great stunt either way—dead or alive."

Alice went into the garage and returned with her Kodak movie camera. She got herself into position and looked through the viewfinder. "Let's roll it!" she said.

Frankie took a paint brush and dipped it into a bowl of gasoline and quickly painted the gauze until it was saturated.

"Showtime!" he called out.

The rules were quickly explained. I was to stand up on the roller skates at the flat top deck of the slide while steadying myself with the bars from the built-in ladder. When Frankie said, "Ready," I was to squat down like a roach and make myself as compact as possible. "Like they do on *Florida Roller Derby*," he said, referencing the popular TV show where skaters raced around a circular track while brutally slugging and kicking each other for points. During the show about half the skaters were taken out on stretchers. It was the cruelest game on TV and I loved watching it, but I wasn't sure about imitating that part of it.

Finally, when Frankie yelled "Set," I made certain that my skates were lined up properly and that I was in my tight, tucked-down position.

Then he held the hula hoop with a pair of grill tongs and pulled out a lighter and flicked it against the hoop. Instantly the flame came to life and chased itself around the gauze. I only had about a second before the hula hoop would melt. As with all of the Pagoda games, there was no room for error but there was a lot of room for disaster and pain and possible lifelong maiming. If I hit the hula hoop the molten plastic would stick to me and burn deeply into my soft flesh and I was sure to be horribly disfigured—something like that melted teddy bear.

As soon as the flame completed its circle Frankie hollered, "Go!" I pushed off the bars and zoomed down the slide.

I think Frankie hollered, "We have liftoff!" as I kept myself tucked down and shot through the middle of the still circular hula hoop while Alice captured it all on film.

Once I lost my momentum my skates dug into the sandy soil and I flew forward and somersaulted over some dog poop. The poop was old and hard so it didn't stick to me.

"I'll get this developed soon," Alice said, sounding very pleased. "Now that we have the movie camera I think we should redo all the Olympic stunts and capture them in movies instead of still pictures."

I couldn't imagine that I would survive another catapult shot over their house and into their pool. This was the right time to change the subject.

"Now can I see the puppies?" I asked. "To pick one out."

"Sure," she said. "But you can only have the sick little runty one."

"What if I don't want the runt?" I said right back.

"So what?" she replied. "Don't be ungrateful when someone gives you something for free."

"I nearly killed myself going through the hula hoop," I argued. "I should pick the one I want."

"With that attitude," she said snottily as her rotating mouth crunched her words into bits, "you won't even get the runt."

"We'll see about that," I snapped. "When Gary gets back he'll straighten this out."

"You are such a gigantic idiot," she continued to crow. "Don't you know that you are *his* runt? He'll put this dud dog out of its misery just like he'll do to you."

At that, Frankie began to laugh uncontrollably as he repeated, "Runt, runt, runt," like he was a grunting pig.

I would have punched him if I didn't deep-down inside think he was insane and would go mental and try to kill me.

I took a few steps toward my house, then turned around and shouted at Alice, "Gary will make you give me one of the good pups. He's my friend!" Of course, my voice shot up an octave, and as I slunk away I tortured myself by hearing my dad mocking me with his "what a panty voice" crack.

FLAMING WALLET

The morning sun was a rising gong of pulsing heat, but I was standing beneath it in the backyard because I knew Gary had come home during the night. It was after midnight when I had heard his whiny complaining to his mother that he needed new underwear before he got married. "Go to Sears in the morning," she had replied.

"You go," he begged her. "You know shopping only gives me itchy fingers."

"Honey," she said sweetly, as if talking softly to a pet, "I'm not going anywhere, but it's traditional to have clean underwear when you get married."

"Then I'll get Frankie to buy them," he said.

So I was up early and standing in my backyard, hosing the dirt and leaves off the back patio and hoping to spot Gary. Since he hadn't gotten married yet I knew he had more time for me.

Finally he did wake up and step outside in some dingy boxers I hadn't seen before. When he saw me he swaggered over to the fence.

"So how'd it go with Leigh?" I asked after turning off the hose and coming over.

"That was one long bad mood," he said, and spit to one side. "So I drive all the way up. I hide the hot tow truck in some woods and walk to Leigh's house trailer. I see her mom and dad, and we solve some old problems. So now I feel real good. Like I found a place in life where I belong, with them and Leigh. Then a little later I borrow Leigh's truck to buy some groceries for dinner, and on the way her older brothers run me off the road and accuse me of stealing Leigh's truck.

"One brother says, 'You don't do something like take her truck without our permission.'

" 'We're gonna be married,' I said. 'What's it matter?'

"Then they flip out and start shoving me and telling me there is no way in hell they'll let Leigh marry me. Honestly, I wanted to kill them, but I just smacked them around a bit.

"So they take her truck and leave me by the side of the road and when I walk back to Leigh's place I tell her what happened. She says her brothers are flipping out about the marriage. 'What's to flip out about?' I said to her. 'I'm going to be family to them, so they should treat me good right from the beginning.'"

"So you didn't get hitched," I concluded, just to keep the conversation alive.

"Not yet," he spat. "So then I had to get the tow truck and chance not getting caught coming back. I ditched it in a parking garage in Pompano Beach and hitched home. We'll just run off as soon as I snatch another car and do it without her family knowing. But right now I need your help."

I perked right up. "Buying underwear?" I replied.

"I don't know who is more nosy—you or my probation officer, who is making another house call this morning," he said.

"How can I help this time?" I asked.

I was eager to do anything I could for Gary because I was nervous about the wallet in my pocket. He wouldn't be happy that Tomi had given it to me and told me the story about where it came from.

"Seems that cop called Mercier about me being suspiciously linked to that missing tow truck," he said. "You got a fix for that?"

"You mean an excuse, right?" I asked.

"Don't make me hurt you," he said, and narrowed his eyes. "I did enough fighting in Alabama—and I'm a smidge away from getting married and off probation—so my mood is fragile."

He held up his scabby fists for me to see what might be coming my way.

"I can tell him that we were on a Sea Cadet training initiation," I suggested. "I already asked my dad, and he said you can join and come on our cadet retreat."

"What kind of training initiation?" he asked.

"Survival stuff," I suggested. "Like spending a weekend in the Glades living off of wildlife and plants."

"I like the survival stuff," he said. "Lots of blood. No telephones. Right?"

"Right," I agreed. "We can tell Mercier we had to toughen up just like we were stranded in real life—like it's training for joining the marines, which we can say you are thinking of doing someday, like following in your dad's footsteps."

"And when's the retreat?" he asked.

"This weekend," I lied, making up the details on the spot. "At Birch State Park on the beach."

"Perfect," he said, and clapped his hands together. "For how long?"

"Two days."

"Excellent," he said, nodding favorably. "I can slip up to Alabama and elope with Leigh and bring her back home. Mercier won't know a thing. Problem solved."

"Not all the problems are solved," I said quietly.

He gave me a puzzled look. "Why?"

"Can I ask you a question?" I asked. "'Cause now I have a problem."

"Don't I usually punch you when you ask me a question?" he said, and cocked his fist back.

"This is more than that," I replied as I reached into my back pocket. I took my time pulling out the wallet and held it straight toward him as if I were revealing the evidence to a crime. "Tomi asked me to give this back to you," I said. Then I stood still and waited for the punch.

"Oh, crap," he said, and took it from me as he glared over at her house. "She's just making trouble like she always does. She thinks I'm going to get pissed off at you, but she's wrong. She probably told you that pathetic story of hers that she tells everyone. I know her backstabbing version backward and forward, and I just bet she wants you to ask me for my side of the story."

"As a matter of fact, yes," I said, feeling slightly relieved that he didn't just haul off and punch me in the face. "That's it exactly."

"And I guess you just stood there like a lovesick puppy and listened to her run me down. Right?" he asked.

I nodded.

"And you didn't defend me?"

"I wasn't sure how to," I said.

"Punch her lights out—like *this*!" he hissed, and hit me so quick and hard on the shoulder I let go of the fence and fell backward on the grass, which was like landing on a bed of nails.

"I'm sorry!" I cried out. "But I didn't want to lie to you about where I got it."

"Save your lies for Mercier," he said. "Don't screw it up for me. Remember, I'm a breath away from freedom."

"Deal," I said, and stood up and stuck out my hand.

He flicked it away. "We're friends," he said. "That's the *real* deal."

"Yeah," I said, trying to mimic his bravado. "So don't worry about Mercier. I can handle him like the last time."

"Okay. That you did." He held up the wallet. "Yeah, I took this off the dead pilot," he stated matter-of-factly. "I risked my life to do it, too, because after the crash he was strapped into his seat and on fire like one of those Buddhist monks. I burned my hands cutting open his flaming jumpsuit and pulling the wallet out of his pants. That's when the spare tank blew and I barely made it out of there.

"I figured I was going to give it to his family rather than let whatever he had in there go up in smoke. Once I opened it was when I saw the thousand bucks. I wasn't sure what to do with it because I don't often find that kind of money. Then right around that time Suzy, who was my girlfriend then, dumped me after she swooped down and stole Tomi's rich boyfriend right off her arm. He was some prep-school kid. Jordan something."

"Abernathy," I added.

"That's it," he said, and snapped his fingers. "Suzy was so money-blind I stupidly gave her the wallet to try and get her back with me. That sure as hell didn't work. I didn't get her back, and she kept the wallet. Then the next thing you know Tomi turns up pregnant. She wasn't my girlfriend anymore. Ask anybody. But mysteriously Tomi ends up with the wallet and the money. So who do you think gave it to her? Suzy? Of course not. But she must have been dumb enough to have shown it to Jordan and he stole the wallet from Suzy and secretly gave it to Tomi, because he was the dirty bird who got her in trouble."

"But why would he do that?" I asked. "Tomi said he was loaded."

"But he wasn't loaded," Gary said, and smiled wryly. "Get this. That Richie Rich act was all a fake. The chauffeur was Jordan's dad, who worked for a limo company. They didn't have a thousand bucks sitting around. And Jordan wasn't sitting around either. After he gave Tomi the wallet nobody saw him again. He vanished. He didn't want any part of those girls, and with the mess he was in he took off to who-knows-where. Hell, I would have run off, too."

"So it wasn't you who got Tomi in trouble?" I slowly dared to ask.

He smirked. "That story she tells about me is a tired old lie. That baby belonged to Jordan, which is why he was so quick to dump her and chase after Suzy. Just think about it for a minute and what I'm saying all makes sense."

I just stood there comparing the two stories like I was in the Garden of Eden wondering if I should bite the snake's apple or not.

"So who are you going to believe? Her?" He pointed to Tomi's house. "She who goes around spreading lies about me? Or are you going to believe me, who has no reason to fear anyone, so I always tell the truth? Why do you think Leigh moved to Alabama? Because Tomi told Leigh's mother I was the dirty bird. No one has a reason to be more pissed at Tomi than me. Being a coward is what makes people lie to themselves and to anyone who will listen to them. I can tell you this—I'm no coward!" He held his swollen red fist up under my chin like it was the apple. "Now," he asked as his rising knuckles lifted me onto my tiptoes, "who are you going to believe?"

Over Gary's shoulder I saw Mr. Mercier's Ford Falcon pull up in the Pagoda driveway. When he got out he glanced toward us and slammed the door behind himself, then pointed to the Pagoda house. "Inside, now!" he hollered like he was scolding a dog.

"Whatever you say to him, make it a winner," Gary whispered, and gave me a quick pat on the back. "Or else you'll be the loser."

I had my work cut out for me because Mr. Mercier was angry and he had his facts together and he started up the moment Gary and I entered the house.

"Somebody ratted you out and let us know you were in Alabama," he said, angrily marching back and forth between what looked like two crushed La-Z-Boy recliners. "Not only is leaving the state without permission a violation, but you were up there harassing your old girlfriend."

"That's not possible," I cut in. "He was with my dad and me on a Sea Cadets trip."

Mercier turned and looked at me as if he could backhand me down the hall. "What are you?" he snapped viciously. "His midget understudy?"

"His friend," I said sincerely.

Detailed lying was my strong suit and by the time I finished telling how Gary and I had gone on a Sea Cadet survival trip and spent forty-eight hours bonding like real men in a raft on Big Cypress Swamp in the Glades with nothing but a flashlight, a paddle, water, and a fishing line, all Mr. Mercier could do was look at Gary with loathing and say, "Well, you didn't seem to get much sun on your sensitive lying face."

"We covered our faces in zinc oxide," I said. "We looked like snowmen—actually snow cones."

I laughed a little at my own joke. It helped strengthen the lie, I thought.

"I think I'm the one being *snowed*," Mr. Mercier said, but he didn't question me any further and before long he looked at his watch and stood up. "I gotta run to court," he said, sounding annoyed. "Believe it or not there are about a million Gary Pagodas out there on the loose, and I'm the guy who has to keep them on a virtuous path—before they end up behind bars living in hell on earth."

After that threat he pointed a finger at Gary. "No funny business," he said. "Or I promise you I'll run out of patience." Then he swiftly turned to me and pulled a pad and pencil out of his jacket pocket. "What's your dad's phone number?"

"We don't have a phone," I replied. "Look in the phone book—no Gantoses in there. We can't afford one."

"Believe me, I'll look," he promised, pointing at me with a menacing glare.

He snatched open the door and walked away without closing it.

After a minute Gary slowly said, "Good job for now. But if he calls, you better pretend to be your father or I could be screwed."

"Don't worry," I said, showing off my cleverness. "We just recently got the phone. It's not listed in the book yet."

Gary flopped down across a recliner. My chess set dropped to the floor and the pieces scattered. Gary reached down and picked up the white king and queen. He held one in each hand, then threw his arm over his eyes.

He looked tired to me, so I took a chance.

“Is this a bad time to talk about the puppy Alice was supposed to give me?” I asked.

“We’ll talk about that later,” he replied. “Right now I’m in a crappy mood and I have to go down to Gus’s and make some phone calls.”

“About what?” I asked.

“Come over here,” he said.

When I did he sat up and slapped me across the face so hard that I staggered toward the wall.

“I owed you that for the last ten questions,” he said, and turned his face away from me. “How many times am I going to have to teach you that?”

“A hundred thousand times,” I said in a hurt voice, then walked out the open door and around to my backyard. I stood there with my cheeks heating up as if I were in purgatory.

Maybe it’s a good day to burn all my clothes, I thought. I had already decided to steal new ones. But then I saw Tomi standing behind her fence. I knew she was waiting just for me.

"Talk to me," she called out in that soft, sweet voice of hers. "You aren't going to let that bully run your life, are you? Come over here and light my cigarette. Come on. I'll blow smoke in your face and give you a kiss and you'll forget all about wanting to be his boyfriend. You'll be my boyfriend. There's a lot more fun on my side of the fence—I promise you that."

I just lowered my head as if those words were a driving rainstorm. I walked blindly forward as she lashed out at me from behind.

"Well," she said loudly, "if you want a little bit of heaven come and see me. But if you gotta go to hell with someone it might as well be him."

That set me on fire.

WORDS OF FIRE

It was Saturday and I was rubbing my mother's sore legs. They were swollen from her standing all morning at the bank. She was a teller and had to wear high heels and now that she was expecting a baby her lower legs had filled with fluid. She was going to quit in a week or two but until then was enduring the swelling to make the extra money.

She was lying back on the couch with her legs up. I was happy to rub them and spend private time with her, but it was always a dangerous time because she could see deeply into the very heart of me and had a way of getting me to tell her what I wanted to hide. We were just too alike.

As soon as I started warming up the skin cream

between my hands she said, "I've noticed some changes in you lately."

"Yeah," I replied. "I'm getting bigger." I held up my right arm and made a muscle. "See?"

She smiled, then continued. "Other changes, too," she said more seriously.

"Like what?" I asked as I pressed on her calves and began to slowly massage them.

"Like you spend all your time lately with that Pagoda boy next door," she replied.

"I'm lucky to have made a new friend," I claimed. "With all our moving I lose friends faster than I can keep them."

"But he seems so much older than you," she remarked in a cautious tone. "His interests might be more *adult*."

"He's only a few years older," I said, honestly not certain how old Gary was. I only knew that he had failed some grades. I didn't know how much time he had spent in juvie, but he was probably three or four years older than me.

"You seem to follow him around a lot," she said. "Is he bossy?"

"A little," I conceded. "But that's just because he's older and used to being his own boss."

"Does he listen to you?" she asked.

"Sometimes," I said.

"May I give you some advice?" she asked.

I really didn't want any. She was going to tell me to "respect myself because if I didn't then no one else would either." She had been saying that most of my life. I was sort of a serial *follower*, so she knew how I operated. Only this time I was older and didn't want to just be a follower. I wanted to be him.

"With Gary I'm sort of the second-in-command," I said proudly.

"The second-in-command is my favorite role," she said in a warm voice. "It's like being a secret boss. The second-in-command can be a good influence and a clever leader by helping to point out the right path to the boss. Like me and your dad. He might be the boss because he's the man of the house, but I'm the leader. I'm the one that gives him good ideas and makes him think he thought of them himself."

That was true. "But is that good enough for you?" I asked.

"Yes," she replied. "Because I know I'm the *real* leader and it's the same for you and Gary. He's the boss, but your job is to put ideas into his head and make him think they are his. That makes you the leader, and then the boss is just a lot of hot air. You see what I mean?"

"Yeah," I said, "but it sounds so complicated. Can't I just follow him like a pal or right-hand man?"

She raised up on one elbow and looked at me with an exasperated expression. Then she lay back against the cushions again and closed her eyes. "You can do a lot better than to be his stooge," she said, which hurt. "You are smarter than that. Stand up for yourself. Just remember, he's the fake boss but you are the real leader."

She'd made that point so many times already I finally got exasperated. "Okay, I got it," I said, and tried to change the subject before she suspected what was really on my mind. I didn't want to be the leader. For now I was the follower, but soon I would be just like him. I'd be his double through and through.

I kept working on my mother's legs until she curled up and fell asleep. Being the leader without being the boss must have been exhausting.

I loved her so much. I looked at her and put my cheek against her upturned hip. I wished I didn't make her life so uneasy, but with the new baby coming she'd worry less about me. I gave her a kiss, then hopped off the couch. Her breathing was labored. I wanted to respect myself like my mother wanted. But when I was alone I had to face who I was—who I really was—and I was so two-faced I couldn't really be alone because each face took turns hating the other. I never told her that. In the past I had told her things about myself that made her cry, and her tears were more unbearable than my own.

I left her side and went into my room. I closed the door and locked it. I felt exhausted with still being the follower. Maybe I was nothing more than Gary's puppy that lived in a shoebox at the foot of his bed. But if I wanted more than that I had to do more than settle for being his runt, as Alice had gleefully said. The runt insult haunted me because I feared it was true. But I had a cure for that.

I knew what I had to do next. I pulled open all my dresser drawers. Most of the clothes I had outgrown, but almost all of them seemed to belong to some other kid that I had rejected. I went through my drawers and scooped out all my socks and underwear and T-shirts. I piled them up on the bed. Then I opened my closet and tossed all my shoes and shirts and pants and a few jackets on top of the others. When I finished I only had one outfit—my shoplifting outfit.

I slipped down to the kitchen and got two plastic trash bags, then returned to my room and filled them equally with the clothes. I slung them over my shoulders and bent over from the weight of them as I marched down the hall. I looked like a runaway who intended never to return, but I was only going to the garage, where I hid them behind some sheets of plywood.

I took a deep breath and when I stepped out of the garage I spotted Gary in his backyard.

"Hey," I called out, and waved that little Tomi King wave before I caught myself and lowered my hand.

"Sailor Jack!" he replied, and walked over to the fence. "You ready to meet some real guys?"

"I'm working at it," I said, and smiled.

"Well, get your motor running because tonight is your night. I have a little initiation in mind that I think you'll like."

"What's that?" I asked.

"Are you asking me a question?" he said, and cocked his fist back behind his head.

"No," I quickly replied. "No questions. Only answers."

He lowered his fist and cracked his knuckles. "See you at the clubhouse," he said, and told me when to show up. "And don't be late."

FAITH IN FLAMES

This next part is the hardest part to tell. Maybe because what I wanted didn't want me. I suppose all of us look at ourselves from time to time and wish we were bigger, stronger, meaner, tougher, and more vicious than the next guy. Being smart just isn't enough. I could be smart on my own at night alone in my room, but I wanted to be fearsome when I was out in the world walking bravely down dark streets or walking indifferently down those blindingly bright school hallways during class breaks. I wanted to be a man, and suspected I wasn't man enough—I wasn't a coward, but I wasn't feared either. Still, I had enough courage to do what I had planned.

First, I hauled my bags of clothes and a can of lighter fluid to the golf course. Gary had told me where there was a tear in the chain-link fence that was hidden by heavy vines. I set them down just inside the fence. I had plenty of time to burn them later. For now, I wanted to get my new clothes before anyone showed up and saw me looking like a kid.

Then I stole the beige Levi's at the Grant's department store. I had walked there in the heat of the afternoon and was so sweaty when I arrived I had to kill time strolling up and down the frozen-food section at the Winn-Dixie grocery store before I settled down and got busy.

I had worn a pair of my baggy khaki work pants to Grant's. I went directly to the Levi's section and selected two pairs that I thought might fit me. I draped them over my arm the way my mother would and carried them into the dressing room. The first pair fit so tight I could just barely get the zipper halfway up. My pinched-in stomach hung over the waistband. *Perfect,* I thought. *They'll stretch into shape.*

I did a few quick deep-knee bends and then sucked in my gut and pulled the waistband together until the large shiny metal stud slipped into the heavily sewn buttonhole. I let out my stomach and the button and hole held tight and didn't pop off. I dragged the zipper the rest of the way up and the teeth didn't separate. I pulled my khakis over them. I returned the second pair to the display where I had found them. A salesgirl casually passed by but seemed to look right through me, as all girls did.

I shrugged. "No luck with the sizing," I said to myself, and stiffly marched straight for the exit. I walked a couple blocks until I felt confident no one was following me and then I quickly peeled the khakis down over my legs and sneakers and threw them in a trash container behind a Burger King.

The shoes were harder to swipe. I stood by the display window and waited until there were no customers in the Thom McAn store. The salesman was a kid not much older than me. I was so new to this area of Fort Lauderdale that no one had ever seen me before. I went in and scanned the display shelf. When I spotted the white alligator pumps I requested my size. When he brought them out I tried them on. Although they fit nicely I said they were "too tight in the toe" and I'd need the next size up. The moment he went into the back storage room I grabbed the shoes. I left the box. I was out the front door in a flash and ran behind the store and cut through a scrubby field toward the back of a Holiday Inn. I put the shoes inside a grocery bag I found by a trash bin and kept walking briskly until I was far enough away from the store. I walked a few streets deep from the main highway, where there was new construction. Inside a half-built house I took the shoes out of the bag and scratched up the soles and heels over a rough concrete threshold in the garage. I grabbed a handful of sandy dirt and slopped it across the toes of the shoes. They were still stiff and smelled new, but they didn't look newly stolen. I put them back in the bag to be on the safe side. So far, it was all so much easier than I had imagined. My heart was pounding and my eyes were darting left and right, but I took a deep breath and kept going.

There was no way I was going to swipe a leather motorcycle jacket from a store. Besides, I wanted a used one that looked more like Gary's, which was all scratched up from taking a few hard spills on a Harley. I didn't want to look like a newly minted gang kid.

I walked down to a church secondhand clothing store called Faith Farm. My parents had bought our furniture there. It was nice—just out of style. The wooden building had been an old Florida hotel, and the donated clothes were sorted by rooms. I started going through a nasty pile of damp leather jackets. There was a lot of mildew on them and they smelled like dead cows in the humidity. The girls' jackets were the same style as the boys', only the sizes were different.

I didn't care. I just needed something to fit into—and by the time Gary's friends arrived at the golf course it would be dark. It didn't take too long to find a guys' leather jacket that was a pretty roughed-up imitation of Gary's. It wasn't much money. I paid them the three bucks and went back to the golf course, where I could put on my new shoes.

I was going to burn my old clothes right away but then thought the smoke might attract someone who would call the fire department. So I took the bags and marched farther in until I found an asphalt path that hadn't fully crumbled into pieces from all the sun, roots, and vines. Gary had said he would meet me at an old clubhouse before it got dark, so I thought I would follow the path. Before too long I found the clubhouse. It was in ruins. Southern oaks had grown through the foundation and collapsed the walls. The moldy terra-cotta roofline sagged like a lower jaw of blackened teeth. Part of the building had been set on fire. Vines laced over the windows like spiderwebs covering flies. The inside walls were velvet curtains of golden-green mold. I ran my hand down the wall. It seemed to purr like a cat. It was a sensation that made me want to live there like a hermit or a monk waiting patiently for the fiery Apocalypse. Unlike my own room, it felt oddly comfortable, surrounded by what had been beautiful, then abandoned and left to rot. It reminded me of my sister's story about being born into perfection and then growing up only to find herself in decline. But she wouldn't be in decline over here. Nature always presses forward to regain its beauty and purity. I missed her at that moment. I wished she was with me so I could tell her that I now understood what she meant when one night she said to me, "The house is a bit of a monster, and slowly you belong to it and begin to function in it like living furniture that gets rearranged—you become another gear inside the machine of the house, or a hand puppet to your parents. You won't find freedom until you find yourself in a place that doesn't own you." She was right about that. And now I felt like a stripped gear that had rolled out of the machine of the house and escaped to find my own special place.

Even Gary had his girlfriend—his girl from Alabama with her white truck and scoop-neck top and rising breasts and blond hair and nice smile and thin lips and an attitude that said she was looking to leave her house with a man and not a boy, looking for some guy who was moody and tough and simple and who loved her completely and wanted out of his house as much as she wanted out of hers.

Just as I wanted to go from the inside of my house to the outside, I wanted to be turned inside out, and so I started taking off the rest of my old clothes. I left my T-shirt on because the leather jacket was still sticky with mildew. I put my new shoes on. There was no mirror, but I didn't need one because how I now felt inside was better than how I could ever look on the outside.

Maybe Gary will see how great it is to be with me, his double, and he won't go up to Alabama and leave me here looking in the mirror at a reflection of myself—that would just be double the misery.

"Hey, Sailor Jack!" Gary hollered. "Where the hell are you?" Startled blackbirds flew up into the air, then resettled. He was over by the fence.

"Over here!" I hollered back. I was very excited for him to see me. He must have been excited, too, because I heard him crashing through the bushes like a beast.

As he entered the clubhouse clearing I spread my legs and arms out like a storefront mannequin. "Notice anything different?" I asked.

"You can look like me, but you aren't me," he replied. Then he stepped toward me and with some malice in his voice said, "I have a bone to pick with you, Sailor Jack."

"Did you bring the other guys?" I asked nervously, looking over his shoulder. I was eager to meet them but didn't want them to see him pushing me around like a kid.

"That's just it," he said. "I had to call off the party because you screwed up with your lousy excuse for Mr. Mercier. He got your phone number, okay."

"But we aren't listed in the phone book," I protested weakly, and felt that this was all about to go the wrong way. "I called the operator and they don't have us listed in information."

"Well, did you ever walk outside your house and look at your dad's company car? His *work* number is in bright red block letters and Mercier wrote them down and called him this afternoon. Your dad told Mercier that there was no cadet survival trip in the Everglades and that you were lying your ass off. So now I am screwed. Mercier called my mom and said it's back to juvie for me."

I didn't figure Mr. Mercier would see the car, and though I was good at lying maybe he was better at catching liars.

"Well, are we still going to have a party?" I stupidly asked. He slapped me hard enough that I fell over and landed across my bags of clothes.

"You deserve that and more," he said, standing over me. "And you'll get more from your dad because he's looking to kick your ass and I've given him a little extra incentive to do so. But for now I got you here with me," he added bitterly, "so I get to kick your ass first."

"What should we do?" I asked, and stood up while keeping my eyes on his hands. "How can I help? Do you want to punish me now and get it over with?" I asked, thinking that if he hit me now he would settle down like a bomb defused.

"If you were me you'd know what to do," he said. "But you aren't me yet, so you don't know. What we're going to do is blast out of here with a bang. I have one final Olympic game for you and then I'm off for Alabama."

"Should I build a bonfire?" I asked. "There's a lot of dry wood and I brought my old clothes to burn."

"Nice outfit," he finally said, calming down a bit as he looked me over.

"I stole everything," I bragged. I didn't mention the jacket.

"Stop showing off," he said, "and get that fire going. Nothing speaks the truth like the pure pain of *flame*!"

I dashed over to where I had the clothes. There was a pit filled with ashes from other bonfires, so I turned my bags inside out and squirted some of my lighter fluid on the old clothes. They caught fire immediately. Then quickly I began to gather up dry branches. I pitched the wood around the clothes as if I were building a tepee. Soon a bright, tall flame shot into the air like the lashing tongue of a snake. As I admired the flames I began to sweat across my chest and down my arms and over my upper lip. It felt good to think about myself as a man.

Gary had walked off as I built the fire and when he returned he had a shoebox in his hand. He set it on the upturned end of a log.

"You know I like games and there is only one tonight—but it is truly life changing," he said seriously. "I call it the Olympic Transformation Game. Kind of a Frankenstein's monster sort of game. Since I only have one box you only have one game choice, but it's better than any three choices combined. All you have to do is lift the top of the box and turn the doorknob and be transformed, and I hang a gold medal around your neck. Simple as sin!"

"What doorknob?" I asked.

He slapped me softly back and forth across the cheeks as if his hand were a paintbrush. "When will you learn to stop asking questions, Sailor Jack?"

I shrugged.

"Let me explain." He opened the shoebox and revealed the runty spaniel puppy. It was as small as a squeeze toy. He lifted it up. "Alice donated it especially for you," he said. "She picked it out herself."

I reached forward and patted its little head. It turned its snout toward me and licked my fingers.

"He is the door you have to open," Gary said, and set him back into the box. "Now put the palm of your hand on his head like it's a doorknob, give it a sharp turn and enter my world."

"This isn't an Olympic game," I said. "You just made this up because you're mad at me."

"Think whatever you want," he replied coldly, "but now it's time to do what you're told to do."

I wavered and looked Gary in the eye.

"After this I'm leaving," he said. "And if you want to step into my shoes, my skin, my wicked ways, you have to open the door and really step *up*. So put your hand back on little Runty's head and turn the knob. Come on, twisting it is no more than opening a tiny dollhouse door."

He reached for my hand and pulled it forward and set it on top of the puppy's head.

"Now get a good grip on it," he instructed. "And turn."

I turned its head to the side and the puppy squirmed.

"I didn't hear it turn all the way," he stated. "It's a door, so you have to turn it hard enough to hear the lock click open. Then you can step forward and call yourself Gary Pagoda. That's what you've wanted, and this is your Olympic moment to transform yourself into me. Now turn the knob because you won't be golden until you open door number one."

"What is your Olympic game?" I asked.

"The Olympic Vanishing Act!" he said proudly. "I'm done here. I'm just going to go up in smoke."

He lit a cigarette. "And since someone has to take my place in juvie when I'm gone it might as well be you—my double. Now turn the knob, snap open the lock, and step into my shoes."

I hesitated.

"Come on," he urged me. "Some of my guys would snap that head off faster than twisting the beer cap off a cold one."

I looked to the side where the flickering light from the fire was casting shadows of my burning clothes inside the empty body of the clubhouse. From the first moment I saw Gary and jumped on his train this was where it led me. Now I was here and this was what I wanted. It was just going to be a little harder than burning my notebooks and shoplifting some clothes. Those acts had been rungs on a ladder to this moment and so I planted my feet and reached forward and held the spaniel's small head in my hand. Then I looked Gary in the eye.

He nodded. "Do it," he whispered. "Go for the gold. You'll never regret it."

I couldn't look at the dog. I looked away from Gary and into the fire, tightened my grip, and turned. The dog's legs scrambled around the box to keep up with the twist of my wrist. I reached forward with my other hand and held his body in place as I turned his head until I reached the point where there was only one small vertebra of resistance. One more twist and I would step out of my space and into Gary's.

He reached forward and pressed his hand over mine. "Time's running out," he said. "The Olympic judges are getting impatient."

Just then the puppy yipped. I jerked my hand away and the box flipped over onto the ground. The puppy rolled out and scurried into the bushes. Gary dropped to his knees and reached down to grab him. The sun had already lowered and the underbrush was dark. I hoped Runty had gotten away. This was all my fault. I had made a mistake about Mr. Mercier but the puppy was innocent. After a minute Gary hopped back up onto his feet. He held Runty in one hand.

"You like fire so much," he said, "so here's a little something to keep it going." He tossed Runty like a log onto the flames.

I spun around and in a few quick steps reached into the fire and snatched him out.

"Loser!" Gary snarled. "Even if you broke his neck you'd never be me."

I lobbed the puppy into the bushes just before Gary's fist caught me on the side of my jaw. I went down onto one knee as he threw his arms triumphantly up over his head.

"Pagoda scores a knockdown in Olympic boxing!" he announced, and did a boxer's shuffle step as he cheered for himself.

That punch had knocked me senseless but I managed to stand back up. His second punch knocked me flat, and this time I stayed down.

"The ref has stopped the fight!" he roared. "It's Olympic gold for Pa-go-da!"

I began to crawl on all fours toward where I had last seen the puppy. Gary lunged at me and landed on my back, locking one hand around my chin and the other on the back of my head. Maybe he'd snap my neck and I'd pass through a door and never come back.

"There is only one reason stopping me from doing what I should," he said, "and she's in Alabama."

He let me loose and hopped up.

"Congratulations," he said bitterly. "Instead of you stepping into my shoes, I've knocked you clean out of yours."

He was right in a way he didn't fully understand. But I did. The more true he had been to himself, the more false I had been to myself.

I rolled over and sat up next to the fire. I felt cold and pulled my smelly jacket over my throbbing head and leaned face forward between my knees. I was frozen in place. Somehow I had slowly transformed, cell by cell and atom by atom, until there were no remains of my own flesh and bone and I'd transformed into a perfect fossil of my own self-deception.

HOUSE ON FIRE

I told you earlier that if you end up not liking yourself then it's better to fake being someone else. The only problem with that advice is sometimes you get tired of being a fake and you want to return to yourself—your true self. I'll tell you this from experience: it's a lot easier to lose yourself inside the maze of someone's life you think is better than your own than it is to stand alone under the noonday sun and be your true self.

So that night he hefted me off the ground and after a few slaps to the back of my head we walked out of the golf course.

When we passed through the fence I saw the half-hidden Rambler in the moonlight.

"That's my dad's car," I gasped. "What's it doing here?" I looked around as if Dad were waiting to snatch me.

"Poetic justice," Gary replied. "Your dad has a big mouth. While he was sitting on your back porch bitching to your mother about what a liar you are, I walked around to the front and rolled the Rambler down the driveway. I had it wired in a minute. Stealing his car is the least I could do to pay him back."

Gary walked directly to the car and got in and started it up.

"But this is my dad's," I said, still not convinced that my dad wasn't lingering in the shadows.

"It still is," he said. "I'll drive it up to Alabama. And you can drive it back to him. End of story."

"I don't have a license!" I exclaimed. "And I don't really know how to drive."

"Sink or swim," he replied. "That's how the pros learned." He shrugged his shoulders as he revved the engine. "Now get in. I can give you a few lessons on the way up, but after that you are on your own."

It was a long drive with few words in between. The water pump squealed like a stuck pig the whole time.

"Why doesn't this piece of junk have a radio?" Gary asked, slapping at the dashboard where a radio would have been placed.

"It's a company car," I said. "No distractions allowed. Do you want to talk?"

"Not really," he said, his eyes shifting back and forth across the rearview mirror as he watched for cops. "Except, why is the engine temperature rising?"

"Pull over," I said. "It's the leaky water pump."

My dad kept two jugs of water in the trunk to fill the radiator when it dropped down to half full and the temperature arm on the dashboard pointed to HOT.

From then on we pulled over at every other gas station and refilled the jugs and kept the water pump working, which in turn kept the engine from seizing up.

We took the Sunshine State Parkway as far as the new exit in Wildwood. From there he knew the two-lane back roads. We drove through the night and into the morning. Eventually we crossed the Florida-Alabama border. Leigh lived in Dothan, not far from there. As he got closer, Gary began to worry about Leigh's brothers and he started talking.

"If I had a gun I'd take care of those brothers," he said. "Does your dad keep one in the glove compartment?"

Not that I knew of, but I checked anyway.

"No," I answered.

"Damn," he said. "I knew I shouldn't have buried those guns in the backyard, but they were dirty."

"You mean they'd be dirty from being buried," I said, correcting him.

He backhanded me the moment I said the last word and just as quickly I could taste blood.

"I don't tolerate idiots who correct me," he growled. "I buried them in the vault."

"What vault?" I asked, and raised a hand to protect my face.

"The vault I buried in the hole I dug. You watched me, you idiot," he said.

"You told me it was a giant Chinese crested," I replied.

"And you were stupid enough to believe it," he remarked.

I almost said, *Well, who is the stupid one now?* but thought better of it.

"Leigh wanted me to bury my past and start fresh with her," he continued.

"And you did it?" I said incredulously.

"Hey, even a guy like me loves nice girls. I guess that's what makes me a parent's nightmare. Huh?"

I didn't answer.

Gary kept his foot on the gas and the water pump was whistling like a train.

"Pull over," I said. "It needs water."

"No. We're almost there," he said.

The water pump howled. The engine was overheating and I could feel the temperature rise through the firewall and under the bottom of the cabin. The floor was so hot I tucked my shoes up onto the seat.

"Pull over!" I said. "The car is going to blow."

But he wouldn't. "Her place is just around the bend," he replied. And it was.

He turned the corner and the moment we pulled up on the front lawn I didn't know if he slammed on the brakes or if the engine seized, but we came to an abrupt stop. Smoke was rolling out from under the hood.

He hopped out and walked with purpose to the front door of a white house trailer.

"Hey, Leigh," he called out, and knocked on the door. "Hey, honey!"

He pushed his hair back to make a nice face when she opened the door. But the door didn't open.

He knocked again.

"It's me," he said. "Gary."

There were no other cars. The windows were barely cracked open. The trailer home looked empty. I noticed the red flag up on the mailbox and walked across the unmowed grass.

"Leigh, it's me," Gary continued. "Open up."

But in his voice I could hear that he was coming to believe something was wrong.

I opened the mailbox, which was nailed to a post, and pulled out a sealed letter with Gary's name on it. Somehow I knew that what was in the letter would hurt him more than all his punches had hurt me. Somehow that cruel thought made me feel better, but smaller too, as if I were my old self again.

"Hey," I hollered across to him. "Mail call."

He half twisted toward me, trying, I'm sure, in those few seconds to imagine what could possibly be in the letter. From the pinched expression on his face he knew it wasn't good.

He ran at me and snatched it from my hand then quickly peeled back the bottom of the envelope. With two fingers like tweezers, he removed a much smaller piece of paper. Maybe it was a lined diary page or just some scrap. I knew it would start on the front side with "Dear Gary." I was standing close enough to read the back, where it ended with larger, looping handwriting: "Love you forever, Leigh."

He read both sides and crushed it in his hand. He returned to the car and retrieved the can of lighter fluid I had used to burn my clothes. Then he marched up to the front door of the trailer. He wrapped his leather jacket around his fist and punched the decorative diamond-shaped glass in the door. It popped out of its frame. He squirted some fluid on Leigh's balled-up letter. Because Alice had dropped his good lighter in the teddy-bear meltdown he pulled out a pack of cheap restaurant matches and lit the letter, then flicked it through the window. Then he went to a side window and smashed the pane and squirted the fluid on the back of an upholstered couch, and across the curtains. Once he set those on fire I knew there was no turning back. He then went around to the other side of the trailer. I heard glass smashing and I figured he continued to do the same.

When he circled back around to where I was standing he finally said to me, "It was those frigging brothers. They snatched her. They're gone. No forwarding address. She said she loves me but it's better that she stick with her family rather than for us to start our own."

It was better for her, I knew. But I didn't say so. And it was probably better for her family. I hoped they were far away. I was glad the Rambler was dead. He couldn't make me drive around with him like a furious maniac while he tried to find them.

And then from his frozen position he yelled out, "Oh, crap!" And he ran for the front door and grabbed the handle. It was already too hot and he jerked his hand back. So he kicked the door in. A rolling ball of orange flames and black smoke curled out the top of the doorway like a bucking bull. The power of the released heat rocked the trailer off its foundation then settled it back down off center.

Gary took a few steps in reverse and caught his breath.

"I want my gift," he cried out. "What I gave her."

Then he lowered his head and charged the open door. He dove in below the belly of heavy flames and smoke and landed on the floor, which was carpeted and steaming from the melting glue and nylon fibers. And then he scurried on his hands and knees around the corner and he was gone down the hallway.

I stood there. Flames roared up like lions and shattered the windows and sent hot shards spinning through the air. I crouched down and kept inching up to the flaming door not knowing what to do. I felt the heat throbbing toward me as I crept forward. I reached out and pawed the air, testing to see how close to the door I could possibly get for when he scrambled back out. But taking a running leap through the flaming mouth of the trailer and down its throat was the path he had chosen, and if I was on his train that was where

I would go, too. I would be in his shoes and pants and jacket, and as his double I would have followed him down that hall and into hell. I'd find him. I'd rescue him. Or I'd die with him.

But I didn't. I leaned forward against the heat until it became too hot to even stand there. I took a step back and shouted his name. "Gary! Get out of there." Then I stepped back and stopped and shouted again. "Get out of there!"

The heat pushed forward and I kept backing up.

The square bathroom air vent on top of the trailer blew off, followed by a thick rope of loopy smoke. It seemed the entire steel trailer frame was sinking down like a ship burning on the water. And then Gary dove through the back window. He rolled on the grass head over heels with the red ends of his hair smoldering like a fuse.

"I got it," he shouted. "It was in her bedroom." He was stretched out on his back in the bright green grass as he held up the white king and queen from my chess set. His eyes were swollen shut. I was by his side and slapping at the winking embers on his smoking pants and jacket, which seemed like they would combust at any moment.

"We were going to be the Olympic king and queen and make all the right moves," he said. "Golden moves."

He reached toward me with the plastic king in one hand and the queen in the other. "Are they melted?" he asked.

They were not, though they seemed unnaturally stuck to his open hands, as if glued to his palms.

His swollen arms were loosely raised above his chest and slowly waving in the air like dancing cobras. I hunkered down onto my knees, trying with my fingers to find some clothing cool enough to grab so I could drag him farther away. I hooked my fingers into his belt loops and tugged him forward. Then, at just the moment I lifted my eyes to look at his blistered arms, the thin pink skin around his wrists detached and rolled slowly down his forearms, like rolling socks, all the way to his elbows. It was like watching snakes shed their skin, and the muscles of his skinless flesh glistened like bloody fillets. I turned when I heard the siren on the fire truck. I waved to the firemen and by the time I lowered my hand they were next to me. One man lifted me up as if I were a puppy and carried me out of harm's way. The rest surrounded Gary and inched him carefully onto a canvas stretcher and carted him off to the arriving ambulance. An EMT held the radio to his mouth while hollering to prep the burn unit for third-degree burns. Then they sped away.

The firemen aimed their hoses on the remains of the trailer home. Soon the flames were beaten back and steam rose like a silver scrim before my eyes, and I knew it was all over and I would never see him again.

The police arrived and questioned me, and afterward they took me down to the station. I answered more questions.

It was easy to be honest about what had happened. Later, after calling my parents and filling them in on the details, the sheriff rented me a room in a small motel.

My dad said it was going to take him a day to get a loaner car from work and drive up to get me.

The motel was named The Crimson Tide after the University of Alabama football team. The rooms were linked together all in a row, like train cars. The office was the engine and the custodian's workshop was the caboose, with a ROLL TIDE flag off the back railing. I had come full circle from jumping onto Gary's train to this. It seemed to be mocking me.

They put me in room 1930. On the outside of the door was stenciled in military letters THE UNDEFEATED TEAM. When the door was closed behind me by the trooper, who had told me not to budge, I did not feel undefeated. I felt beaten. I glanced over my shoulder. There was a giant stuffed red elephant on the bed. If I had a match I think I might have set it on fire.

I suppose if I really had become like Gary I'd have destroyed myself as he was doing, but I wasn't him. Nor was I his angelic opposite—a "good" version of him.

It was just me all along playing at being his imaginary friend. It was a kid's game and I was old enough to know I couldn't reshape myself into him, but I was so bored with my life I took a chance at trying to be someone else.

In a day or so I had been brought home. I tried to go back to being myself. I sat in my room and attempted to read, but my tears fell onto the page as if the words were storm clouds hanging darkly over every thought. It seems I was full of sadness. My mother could see it in me and so she helped and we soon moved to another neighborhood. But the trouble came with me like an ember, and it burned slowly, and hid cleverly enough to where I couldn't feel it, and by the time it flared up again it was too late to put it out, and once more I followed in the shadow of someone else.

AFTERWORD

The car ride back to Florida with my dad was as bad as you can imagine.

First, we went to the junkyard to take insurance photos of his company car because the engine had seized up and the car was totaled. We popped the trunk open and transferred all his concrete sample books into his new company car—a Rambler American, which was the cheapest model they made and a demotion for my father.

After that he asked me what had happened and I told him all about Gary and Leigh and the fire—but not everything. I didn't tell him about my inner life and how I had wanted to be Gary. I kept that to myself, locked up in my heart, or thought I had. This is what I remember most clearly about the trip home because it's the truth that always sticks its knife in you the deepest: We were driving in the slow lane because of the lousy car when he glanced at me and said, "I suppose you think you are a great individualist dressed in that getup like some kind of punk antihero. But you are nothing but a common conformist like all the other Pagoda wannabes that are a dime a dozen."

I never answered him. Not properly. How can you reply to something like that when you feel dead inside from just having the fire in your heart reduced to ashes?

Instead I said, "I hate myself."

He glanced over at me with a look of bewilderment on his face.

After a minute or so he said, "You should join the navy when you turn eighteen. It'll make a man out of you."

"I think I'm doing pretty good on my own," I replied.

After that we traveled in silence.

At home I quit the Sea Cadets. I avoided my family. And after we moved, nothing really changed for me. I stayed holed up in my room. I imagine Gary probably returned to his old self, but I did not go back to being my old self. What trouble was in me hardened and stayed under my skin, even though I realized I was neither cruel enough nor sentimental enough to be him.

Soon the excitement over Mom's new baby kept the spotlight off me, which was a good thing. At my new school I didn't join the chess club or the Latin club as before. I kept slipping out of class and hiding in empty rooms. When I did make a run for the exit I had to pass the school's trophy case. I noticed there was no trophy moment for lost kids like me who'd rather win a Pagoda Olympics gold medal for nearly killing myself than a school sports event that bored me to tears.

By the time I made it into high school I didn't care what might next happen to me. My life was never my own, so I abused it because it wasn't the one I wanted. I don't know what happened to Gary—after the hospital he got sent back to juvie. He probably ended up in prison. His life was never his own either because no one would allow him to live it his way.

I dropped out of school and again moved with my parents, this time to Puerto Rico, where I worked on a hotel construction project with my father. The work didn't unite us. We didn't see eye to eye on much.

I quit and returned to school in Florida, where I moved in with a family who rented me an extra bedroom. They were friendly. They treated me well, but

I wasn't interested in pulling myself together when all along it was my goal to escape my parents and then become someone I loathed more than someone I loved. It didn't take long for me to be a smart-ass to the nice family and make a mess of their home life, so I moved out. But soon I landed on my feet and was living by myself in a welfare motel and making all my own decisions. That was a breath of fresh air.

At last I was in charge. I could choose my own future.

But while I was waiting around to make a choice, I did what I always did and found someone to make a choice for me. I met some nice guys and they had a plan to make a ton of quick money. They were just missing one piece of the plan to make it all happen, and since I had always been a piece of someone else's plan I once again fit right in. I wanted to be just like them and that led to another disaster, which released the trouble already lurking within me. If you read *Hole in My Life*, you'll see what I mean.